The Enchanted Christmas Cottage

By Jeanna Lowry

Dedications

God is the guide of my daily life and is the basis for my faith. My family gives me my inspiration every day. My husband has been by my side for forty years. Adoption blessed us with our son. They both support me in my retirement adventure and encourage me daily. Always with a positive attitude and love. I can't thank them enough for always being there for me. I love you both so very much. Thank you with all my heart and love.

Acknowledgments

To my unconventional adopted family of 10. A chance meeting at church and an invite to dinner. We became instant family. Thank you for the editing help and the girl power time for writing. Between all the texting and phone calls, we did it. I wrote something my entire family can enjoy reading. Thank you with all my love

Contents

CHAPTER ONE

It was December 16th. James was sitting on the couch in his office with a cup of green tea, with honey and a little vanilla flavored cream, sipping from his favorite mug. It was no ordinary mug. He had received it as a gift for the first anniversary of his business. The logo and the name of his company were printed on it.

It was an ordinary day; he was looking out the window at the beautiful mountains of Colorado. The view charmed him so much that he was lost in it, not able to think straight.

After a moment, he heard some noise that turned his thoughts back in time. James was back on campus after Christmas break with his family. His first class of English Poetry was in the theatrical complex on the far side of the campus. This complex had several stage areas with theater seating.

It had been snowing heavily since early that morning. James was reluctant to leave the comfort of his warm room. It was, in actuality, more appealing than the harsh cold and snowy winds outside. He decided it wouldn't be good to miss the first class, so he walked through the storm to the complex. As James entered through the crowded door, he found a spot to move freely. It was much warmer inside, and his body no longer felt numb.

James stepped back and bumped into someone while removing his snow-covered coat. Without turning to look, he said, "I'm sorry."

"That's ok," a soft, calm voice of a girl responded, right before she walked off. He never saw her face; only her long black flowing hair and a scent of vanilla lingered in the air as she walked away.

James hurried to follow her. He slipped into the classroom behind her and noticed it was the same class he was supposed to be in. By the time he had arrived, most of the students were already settled into their seats. James scanned the room to find where she was sitting. Just as he spotted her, he found a seat close enough but at an angle where he could look over and see her properly.

James was a thin, six foot one inch, red-headed, freckled face, 23-year-old, with green eyes. He was lean, but he had a charming personality. From what he could see at a distance, she was a gorgeous girl with coal-black hair. After she turned her head a couple of times, he was able to catch a few glimpses of her face. James thought she looked fit to be an angel with dark eyes to match.

For the next two weeks, he watched her in class. James wondered if he should say hello. *Would she even talk to him, or would she think he was strange like his closest friends did? Would she be scared of him? Had she noticed that he had watched her for two weeks, how would she react to him?*

It was Friday, and at the end of the class, James decided it was time to say hello and test his luck. He could no longer bear to see her from afar. For once, he wanted to make acquaintance with her, at the very least. He walked over to where she was sitting. He stood still like a wooden toy soldier and grinned. He couldn't move, and he couldn't get himself to say a word. It took him a lot of courage to walk up to her, but now that she was right in front of him, he felt awkward standing there.

She looked up at him as soon as she figured that someone was standing.

"Hello," she said in the sweetest voice he had ever heard.

He melted like butter and felt weak in the knees. *Why would God give anyone such a soothing voice?* James was stunned, as though he had just seen an ethereal being. He had lost his voice somewhere inside him. He cleared his throat and tried to compose himself.

"Hello. Can I walk with you today?" James asked instantly and continued speaking.

"I'm James, James Lucks."

He caught himself getting ready to put his hand out for a handshake. Luck sided with him because she looked down to grab her books and never saw him fumble.

"Yes, I would like that. I'm Jenny Benjamin; nice to meet you."

Wow, she's beautiful and polite. She seems like a friendly person.

James then asked her, "Do you have enough time to get something to drink at the cafe before your next class?"

"Yes, actually… I do," Jenny replied.

"Green tea with honey is my favorite. My next class is here in the complex and not for an hour," she added right after she agreed and walked towards the café.

She made it easy for James to talk to her, and she was reasonably approachable, unlike many of the pretentious women found on this campus. James followed her lead, found a table, and sat down.

"My next class is Theatrical Writing," Jenny revealed.

"Yes, I thought so. I'm in that class too."

"Yes, I know you are," she teased.

"Oh no," he said with a shy smile, "I'm busted."

"That's ok. I've noticed you too," she added.

"Whew," James said, "I thought you wouldn't even talk to me. Thank you."

Jenny grinned as she looked into his eyes.

"What do you think of our professor?" James asked. He wanted the conversation to continue. He wanted Jenny to keep talking and never stop soothing him with her calming voice.

"Well… he is brilliant; I'll give him that, but a little off the wall."

"I agree," he said.

I don't just agree; I love her response. She's insightful and opinionated. I like that!

James excused himself and went to the cafe counter and ordered two green teas, both with honey and one with a touch of vanilla cream. Jenny looked around the cafe's court. It mainly was all windows, with access to a beautiful outdoor courtyard buried in snow. The aroma of fresh coffee and tea was bold and filled the air. One half of the court was a cafe, and the other was a deli and pizza counter. The smell of hot pizza dough came from the ovens and mixed with the aroma of coffee and tea. That was enough to make anyone hungry. The seating area was set up for students to study as well.

While Jenny observed her surroundings, James arrived back at the table with their tea. He was exuberant to tell her that green tea was his favorite, but he liked adding a little vanilla cream. Jenny asked for a sip to taste, and he gladly handed her his cup.

"Uhm," she said. "It smells very nice and is tasty too." She handed the cup back to him. "Thank you, but I like mine better," she boasted.

They both laughed in unison.

"Would you sit with me in class today?" he asked.

"Yes," she replied, "That would be nice."

James pulled out his class schedule, "Shall we check to see if we have any other classes together?"

Jenny said jokingly, "Oh, you mean to say you don't know all my classes already."

James nervously responded, "I might."

They both chuckled and looked at the schedule. They had three out of four classes together. So far, everything went quite smoothly, and the two seemed to get along pretty well. It was only their first interaction, but their wavelengths matched, and they were talking as though they had known each other since childhood. James tried to hold back his excitement as he knew they both had the chemistry he was looking for.

"Wow, maybe we could be study partners if that's ok with you," he said, but his voice trailed off as he continued, "Actually, I'm sorry, I'm not trying to be pushy."

Jenny replied immediately, "No, no, don't be silly. It would be nice to study with you. Maybe tomorrow we can study for the Advanced American Literature class exam, and maybe next week we can team up for the English Poetry class."

"Yes! Yes! Let's do it!" James said.

Jenny told James she was sure they would do well in class together.

James boasted in a goofy voice, "I'm sure we'll make the best team in the poetry class. We'll have the best collection of poems."

Jenny pulled the list of required poems needing to be written for the class out of her bag. Drama, comedy, mystery, happiness, and love. Five poems total were due for the course.

"We have one week to turn in our first poem. We can choose the order we will work in," James said.

Jenny nodded and looked up at the clock, saying, "We better go, or we'll be late for class."

As they walked to class, James asked, "What year are you?"

"I'm a junior, and what year are you?" she asked him.

James replied, "I'm a junior also. I know I will graduate next year, but I haven't decided what I want to do yet; I do know I want to be in business for myself."

Jenny responded, "I'd like to be a teacher or a writer."

James said, "My parents think I should have a clear path laid out for myself already."

"I don't think anyone should rush and make a hasty decision about something as important as one's career. We still have a year, and you need to love what you do to be good at it."

James nodded as they walked on.

"Shhh," Jenny said abruptly as she put her finger to her lips. It was dark as they walked into the classroom. The instructor was on stage with a spotlight lighting him up. As they scanned the stage, they realized the instructor was in a full Victorian costume. They hurried to find seats they could sit on as most of them were already filled. Everyone was whispering as they squeezed and squirmed by. He walked off stage without saying a word. As they found their spot, they sat quickly. Jenny started to giggle a little. James poked her with his elbow.

"Behave yourself," he whispered in her ear.

The stage props appeared to be ready for the play. "Well, this is a theatrical writing class; maybe this is our theme today," Jenny murmured.

A castle and a stone wall were laid out on one side of the stage, while a boat lay in the middle. On the far side was a fake village. The themed set went completely dark for a few seconds, the spotlight came back on, and there the instructor stood.

"Hello, class," he said in a slow, deep, drawn-out voice.

In perfect unison, the class replied, "Hello, professor."

Jenny started to chuckle and asked, "Did you hear the way he said hello?"

"Yes," James replied in a low, slow, drawn-out voice. Then he gave Jenny a funny look and started to laugh. She could hardly stay quiet with her giggles and covered her mouth to prevent her laughter from being heard. She was playful and funny and made the class that was rather dull bearable. The professor instructed the class to write a one-act play after witnessing what was going on stage and later on turn it in at the end of class that day.

James got excited; he personally loved the task.

Both of them finished their assignments at the same time. James grabbed Jenny's paper and turned them both in.

After they were done with the class, Jenny and James made their way back to the cafe area and got another table. It was still snowing pretty heavily outside, and they knew a change of plan was in order. They pulled out their books and decided to stay and study there.

"Do you ski?" James asked.

"Not very well, just a beginner. I am from Florida, and we have no snow there. My parents have only been here a couple of times. They're not fond of the cold. I chose a school in Chicago to experience snow and weather changes. I loved it, so I stayed. Plus, I am enjoying the city life here."

She glowed when she spoke about the things she loved, and James enjoyed listening to her.

They talked about everything that day. She told him about her summer job at a bookstore and that she still works there part-time. James told her about the bakery he works for part-time on weekends. One thing led to the

other, which prolonged their conversation. He bragged
about their fantastic cinnamon rolls while Jenny flaunted
all she knew about books.

"Oh, you must work at Marcos Bakery. They do
have the best cinnamon rolls I have ever tasted. I love to go
in on Sunday mornings and get them hot out of the oven.
I'll have to shout at you next time I'm there," Jenny said.

***

James was done with classes for the day. It was time
for Jenny's next class. A month had passed to their first
encounter. They had been spending every day together
since then. James knew it was time to tell Jenny how he
really felt about her. For the occasion, James had made a
beautiful dinner. It was Valentine's Day, so he bought
white and red roses. Before they got to eat dinner, James
was pale with nervousness. He wanted to wait till after
they got done with their dinner, but he blurted out
abruptly, "I love you! I've loved you from the moment I
bumped into you. All I wanted to do since then was to
spend my time with you. And all I want to do in the future
is to spend the rest of my life with you!"

Jenny blushed and smiled. She didn't know what to say as James caught her in the moment.

"I love you too," she said, overwhelmed with emotions. She had felt the same but didn't have the courage to admit it. But now that James had expressed how he felt towards her, there was no reason for her to keep her feelings a secret.

"From that first cup of tea, where we shared a sip as total strangers, I knew you were special."

And just like that, for the next two months, they were inseparable.

CHAPTER TWO

A knock at his door interrupted the time that he wanted to spend in silence. He heard a knock at the door, and came back to reality and found Jack, his brother, at the door.

"Come in, Jack," he said.

"Hey, little brother, would you sign these papers, please?"

"Yes, of course," James said as he got up and walked to his desk.

Jack said as he scanned the room, "I see you have grandmother's ceramic tree out and no other decorations for Christmas."

James replied, "Yes, and that's all that will be out in my office. Here are the papers," he handed them back to Jack.

"Thanks," Jack said as he left the room, shutting the door behind him. James looked up at the shut door and looked around the empty room.

He found himself smiling as he sat comfortably at his desk. His dissociated mind drifted him to the past.

***

"Oh, Jenny," he said, "I remember."

It was the last day of the theatrical writing class. James and Jenny had partnered up in the final project, and it was time to turn it in. James had a one-act monologue play to read, so he excused himself to go to the stage area. His was the last one in class to be done. Jenny had done hers the week prior. She quickly found her seat right up front, in the middle. Jenny wanted to hear every word coming out of his mouth. She had grown so deeply in love with James. Her face and eyes lit up as she looked up at the stage.

The lights went dim, and everyone started clapping. Jenny was cheering as well. The curtain pulled apart, and there stood James. The crowd settled down, and James began his words with, "I met the love of my life when I bumped into her by chance." A puzzled look stretched out on Jenny's face as she sat back in her chair. *It sounded like our story*, she thought. *This wasn't the monologue we wrote together. Is he about to tell everyone?* She asked herself. She listened to their story told by the only person she trusted to tell it. He described every detail with passionate fun and vigor. After a deep breath and a pause, he pointed at Jenny and announced to the entire audience that she was his true love and the reason for the story. Jenny teared up as she put her hands together and blew him a kiss. Cheers, whistles, and clapping came resounding from the class. He asked her to come up on stage. She bashfully crouched down in her seat, smiled, and mouthed the words "I love you." He then motioned for her to join him, "Come up here with me," he said. She nodded and reluctantly went up on stage.

The class started to encourage and cheer her as she made her way to the stage. They were about to be the darling couple everyone on the campus adored.

"What are you doing?" she asked in a very soft voice. "James, this is a one-person play," she reminded him.

James dropped to one knee, and a complete hush came over the auditorium. He declared his love for her, and with tears in his eyes, he asked, "Will you marry me?" As he opened up a little red box, "please" was the next word that came out of his mouth, loud and clear. The roar of laughter came over the dark auditorium.

Jenny chuckled and covered her face with her hands in total surprise. She gasped and started to cry and then began to shake all over.

"Yes, yes!" Jenny answered between the tears. Yelling and applause came from the class as they gave them a standing ovation. She held out her left hand, and he put the ring on her finger. He stood up, hugged her, and yelled, "Let's get married at Christmas!"

Jenny asked, "Which Christmas?"

"This year, of course," he said.

Jenny laughed, threw her arms in the air, and shouted, "Why not? We graduate on the third of December. I believe we can work it out."

Just as they reached a consensus, they hugged, and the curtains closed. She kissed James passionately as soon as they were away from the audience's sight.

Jenny asked out of curiosity, "Did everyone know about this except me?"

James didn't respond, but his eyes searched around and met with the professor, who was smiling ear to ear.

The professor walked up to them, and told Jenny as he winked at James, "We can keep a secret, you know." He turned to James and patted him on his back as he said, "Well done."

"Thank you, professor. It was better than I could have ever imagined," James said.

It wouldn't have been possible without the approval from the professor and the support he showed

Jenny was overcome with emotions, and she tearfully said, "Thank you so very much, professor. I had no idea. It was the greatest surprise ever."

James and Jenny left the stage holding hands. After gathering up their books, James asked Jenny to get a cup of hot tea from the cafe.

"Yes, let's take a few minutes so I can gather my nerves," she said as she calmed herself down.

Jenny found a table, and James carried the drinks and joined her. "We have six months to plan it all," Jenny said, counting the months on her finger.

"Yes, why wait? We'll have the snow we love, and it will be perfect." James replied.

"What day in December do you want?" Jenny asked.

"How about close to Christmas? For the color, I thought we could do red." James said with much enthusiasm.

Some of the classmates walking past stopped to congratulate them and told them how special, and unique the proposal was.

Jenny's phone began to ring, "Oh, it's my parents. I need to get this." She picked up the call and said into the phone, "Hello, mom and dad."

"Did you say yes?" her dad screamed into the phone.

"Yes, I did," Jenny replied. She put the phone on speaker so James could listen to them as well.

"When did you tell my parents?" She asked James in a shocked tone.

Before James could answer, her dad said quickly, "Ah well, James called last week and asked for permission. I was happy to tell him to take you off my hands."

"Daddy!" Jenny responded, "You did not?"

"Nah," her dad said jokingly, "Congratulations, baby girl. We love you."

Her mom chimed in, asking, "When can we see the ring, please? When is the wedding? I'm so excited to help you plan."

Before Jenny could answer, James' phone started to ring. It was his parents' calling. Jenny let out a chuckle as he also put them on speaker.

"Hello, mom and dad," he said into the phone.

His mom squealed in, "Did she say yes?"

"Hello, mom! Yes, I did," Jenny answered.

"Oh! Great!" James' mom shouted!

"While we have all of you on the phone together, we'd like to share our plans. This December, after we graduate before Christmas, we plan to get married," James announced in a loud voice.

Both parents started cheering with excitement. It was happening all too fast, but whatever was happening, it was for the best. Jenny's mom asked, "Where's the wedding going to be?"

Jenny said, "We'd like to do it here, but we haven't decided that yet. I just said yes an hour ago."

Jenny's dad responded with the same vigor, "You know I'll freeze."

In her sweet, melodious tone, Jenny replied, "Aww, daddy, you can handle it."

"Anything for you. I love you, my baby girl!"

Over the phone, James' dad communicated to Jenny's dad, asking him to wear a coat. They both started laughing at his tone.

James reminded them about the little church he once saw on campus. From the time he laid eyes on it, he had hoped to get married there.

Jenny responded, "Oh, that would be nice. It's a beautiful church indeed. We only want a small private family function, something very intimate and private."

James agreed as he wanted nothing big either.

Jenny's mom asked, "Would you all like to come to Florida this summer? I really want to meet you all. We have plenty of room, and no one needs a hotel. We're family now!"

The enthusiasm in the voice of James' mom was evident as she replied, "Yes, we'd love to come."

Jenny's mom and dad started yelling with excitement. They had so many questions, and they started shooting them over the phone, one after the other.

"When, tomorrow? How about today?" Jenny's dad asked in a teasing tone. They all laughed in unison.

Jenny's mom asked if there was a place close by that could help with a small reception.

"Even a restaurant," she said, "Someplace you both like."

Jenny thought for a moment before she said, "I believe we know of a place, 25-30 people could fit nicely," and she was grateful for the help.

"It's an Italian restaurant. We all like Italian food," she said.

James' mom asked if it was the place they went to eat while visiting them about a month ago.

"Yes," Jenny affirmed.

James' dad said, "We loved that place, the food is so good, and they are generous with portions."

Jenny's mom agreed as well, "It sounds good to us." Both moms decided it was time to go as the call had already prolonged. They started blowing kisses to the darling couple. Once again, Jenny was overcome with emotions. She teared up a little after seeing both their families getting along so well.

"Miss you so much," Jenny told her mom and dad. "See you soon, son," James' dad was heard saying before they all hung up.

Jenny turned to James and asked, "Are you sure about me, and do you still want to get married this soon?"

"Oh, yes," James said proudly, "I'd marry you today if I thought you would, but I know you need time."

James was right; there was no need to rush. Like all the other girls, she had some plans for the wedding. Even if they wanted their wedding to be an intimate event, they still needed to prepare accordingly.

"I guess we better check with Giovanni's Restaurant to see if Roberto has room for us in the party room," Jenny said.

James stood up and recommended, "They go there tonight to celebrate."

"I better hurry to my last class before summer break begins," Jenny said as she grabbed her books. James teased her that his classes were all done now, and that he was free to do all the things he had planned on doing. He told her he would make a reservation for dinner that night. He held Jenny's face in both his hands and gave her a big loving kiss before Jenny ran off to her class.

Did she just shy away from me?

James yelled to her, "I love you forever!"

That evening, when Jenny got free from her class, the couple went to Giovanni's, sat at a table, and asked to see Roberto Giovanni, the owner of the restaurant. They had become good friends over time.

They waited patiently and talked about the future while waiting for him to arrive. When Roberto arrived at the table, they asked him to sit with them for a minute. They shared the big news with him. He stood up.

"Meraviglioso! Wonderful!" he shouted, with his arms in the air.

He clapped his hands together in excitement and embraced both of them in his arms. Roberto always mixed some of his words with Italian, especially when he was happy, and that was most of the time. He was a cheerful man with a vibrant personality.

Roberto was so delighted and excited for them that he announced their news to the entire restaurant. He said that if something good happens, it is better to share happiness with others. That was his way of spreading happiness across the room, and he did that effortlessly.

People they didn't even know came up and congratulated them. A couple even paid for their dinner that night as a congratulatory gift. It was nothing less than a little celebration to honor their engagement.

Jenny and James were so grateful for Roberto, but there was something they still had to discuss. Roberto finally sat with them again and asked when the big day was.

"Can I please get an invite?" Roberto said jokingly.

"That's why we're here. We would like to have a small family reception here."

James broke the news to him. The couple wanted to see his reaction. Of course, he'd be more than happy to offer them the place. And their prediction was right. As soon as he heard about it, Roberto clapped his hands and danced in his chair with excitement.

"Yes, yes, of course. When is the big day?" he asked as he settled back down.

"Well," James said very slowly. Jenny just blurted it out "In December this year, if possible. Please."

Jenny smiled and looked Roberto in the eyes. "Can you help us?" Jenny asked.

"Oh, Jenny," Roberto said. "Let me get my planner." He ran off to the hostess station.

Jenny leaned over and snuggled into James' arms. James pulled her closer to him and said, "I love you." Jenny looked up at James with her dark eyes twinkling in the dim lighting as she said, "I love you too." Roberto returned with the book in his hand.

"Wow Jenny, per te la mia dolcezza," he said opening the book.

James translated, "For you, my sweet one."

Jenny replied, "Grazie" "Thank you, Roberto." Roberto nodded and said, "Looks like we're fully booked from December 21st through the Christmas Eve. I have most bookings during weeknights before the 21st because it's for business parties."

"I knew this was a popular place because the food is so good," James said with disappointment.

"A lot of people book for their next year's party the night of their current party. Un Momento, one moment, looks like Saturday, December 18th… is ok," Roberto finally uttered.

James looked into Jenny's eyes, and she melted as he asked her if she wanted to get married on a Saturday.

"December 18th," Roberto repeated, "It's good, in my book."

"Saturday would be perfect. We can spend Sunday with our families before they all return home," Jenny said. She was literally blushing at this point, not knowing what to say further, she just looked down at the calendar.

"Perfect," Roberto said, "So Saturday, December 18th."

Jenny and James replied in unison, "Yes."

Roberto instantly started scribbling in his book to save the date. Jenny also told him that they would like to get a menu from him but that they thought they'd enjoy a trio meal for everyone. Lasagna, chicken parmesan, alfredo, and a salad with bread. That's what they had in mind. It was the perfect meal, and they both personally enjoyed it too.

"So, family style or plated?" Roberto confirmed.

"Oh, plated for sure," said James.

Jenny then asked if Marco's Bakery could make the wedding cake for them.

"Oh yes," Roberto replied. "You know he is my cousin; he'll do a good job for you."

"I work there part-time," James chimed in to inform, just in case Roberto wasn't aware.

Roberto yelled "Molto bene…very well. The very best Tiramisu in the world, my cousin knows how to bake, he can cook too, but bake, ahh…fantastico!"

He paused for a bit, controlled his excitement then said, "Let's go look at the room."

"Percorrere…come, come," Roberto motioned to them.

They both got up and followed Roberto through a massive hand-carved door. It was shaped round like a wine barrel. The room was beautiful at every turn. Scenic paintings adorned the walls, and grapes were hanging from the ceiling. There was even a beautiful water fountain in the one corners of the room, and the floor had beautiful marble tiles laid down.

"It looks like we're in Italy," James said.

"I know, right? It's majestic!" Jenny's eyes were open wide as she gazed around the hall carefully.

Roberto told them they would move all the tables into a horseshoe shape so the bride and groom can be seated in the center.

"It's perfect," Jenny said.

Once again, she started to tear up. It held considerable importance for her to look at the place she would tie the knot with the love of her life. She just couldn't hold in the lot of emotions brewing inside her.

Roberto hugged her and repeated the words "Per te la mia dolcezza, for you my sweet one."

Roberto assured them he would decorate the room in accordance with the Christmas theme.

"White tablecloths and red napkins, don't you worry," Roberto said.

"Wonderful, we won't have to decorate, and those are our colors," Jenny said.

They had talked about most of the decorations and arrangements that needed to be done for their wedding. They returned to their table once again, and ordered food for themselves as they were starving at this point.

After dinner, Jenny and James called their parents from the restaurant. They wanted their families to be the first ones to know about the wedding venue. They told them the date and all their decisions regarding the arrangement.

Of course, they still needed to go to the chapel and ask for availability for that day.

"When they come to Florida, James could you please bring your parents so they we can all meet and the girls could shop for their wedding dresses," Jenny's family stated.

Jenny and James agreed to visit during the second week in June. Jenny was taking one online class, but she said she could squeeze some time that week. They decided to drive because all four of them could share the task of driving.

Their families truly made their lives easy as they all pitched in to help with something. James' mom owned a flower shop outside the city, and she offered to do the flowers.

When everything was finally coming together, James went to the church on campus on Monday morning, and booked the date for the wedding and its rehearsal. He made sure to inform them that the decorations in the church would be red and white poinsettias – perfect for the wedding!

CHAPTER THREE

That second week of June came so fast. Everyone piled into James' dad's car for the trip. It was comfortable with lots of room, so everyone was able to fit in. The drive was pleasant, and it was only one night in a hotel.

After spending a night at a hotel, they finally got to Jenny's house. James' dad stepped back and took a long look, "This is quite a beautiful place, Jenny," he declared.

Jenny said, "Thank you, we've been living here for about twenty years now; I was young when we moved here."

Jenny's parents came running out, and her mom was yelling, "They're here, they're here!" Her arms opened as she grabbed Jenny and wrapped them around her, "Oh my girl, I have missed you!" She walked up to James and hugged him "Hello, son, that sounds so nice," she said. "I'm Susan; just call me mom."

She walked up to James' mom and hugged her; she said, "I'm Susan Benjamin." The excitement of the wedding was apparent; Jenny's mother just couldn't hold it in.

James' mom replied, "I'm Brenda Lucks."

"I'm so happy you're here, so glad to meet you finally," Susan replied with a wide grin.

She made sure to give them a warm welcome, and to make them feel at home.

Jenny's dad went to James right away, hugged him, and said, "Thank you for loving my baby girl; just call me dad."

Jenny's dad went up to James' dad and shook his hand, "Nice to finally meet you face to face. I'm Sam Benjamin."

James' dad put his non-shaking hand to Sam's shoulder and said, "I'm Matthew, just call me Mat like everyone does."

Susan took Brenda and introduced her to Sam, and Matthew introduced himself to Susan.

Jenny walked up to James and said, "Look, you'd think we've all known each other for years."

James squeezed Jenny close to him. They were busy kissing when the parents all chimed in together.

"Hey, save it for later," Matt yelled the loudest. Susan suggested they get the bags and go inside. The men grabbed the bags, and while they were all walking toward the door, the mothers were busy chatting about how great it was to finally meet. They were looking forward to their plans to help with the wedding.

Jenny grabbed James' hand and said, "Come, let me show you your rooms."

Up the stairs, they ran. Sam and Mat followed with the bags. Jenny was busy showing James their rooms when Susan yelled upstairs that ice tea would be out at the pool. Jenny and her dad stopped for a private moment on the way to the pool patio.

Jenny hugged her dad and said, "I love you, daddy."

"Are you happy, my darling daughter?"

"Oh yes, dad," she replied.

"Was it a total surprise?" he asked. "James called and told us his plans, and it sounded creative."

"Daddy," she said, "He never let on, I knew nothing, it was amazing, but everyone else knew. For a long time, I knew I would be with him forever. After he told me he loved me, that's when I knew. Dad, he's wonderful, and I love him."

"Baby girl," Sam responded, "That's all your mother, and I've ever wanted for you."

"His parents are very nice; they treat me well; I hope you and mom like them."

They started walking to the pool patio to join the rest after having a heart-to-heart. Something inside Sam was finally at peace now, maybe it was the feeling of having his daughter in safe hands, but he was finally content at what life had in store for his baby girl.

Everyone seemed to be having a great time. James stood up as Jenny got closer. He leaned over and kissed her cheek. He made room for her to sit next to him on the wicker loveseat.

Jenny asked casually, "Mom and dad will you be ok with coming to Chicago for the wedding? In cold December?"

"Your dad and I would go to the ends of the earth for you. We're so excited that you included us in the planning."

"Why wouldn't we?" Jenny caressed her mother's hands.

"We're keeping it simple, though," The couple said simultaneously.

"Very simple, mom," Jenny added. She told them Brenda owns a flower shop and that she is doing the flowers. They also told them everything about the venue and how helpful Roberto had been to them.

Susan announced, "We have an appointment at the bridal shop tomorrow."

She turned to Brenda and said, "I hope you want to come, I took the liberty to make appointment for all four of us."

"Oh Jenny, your cousin Debrah is coming. She would like to get a dress you choose for her," Susan added, "I hope you don't mind her coming too."

Jenny said very, very excitedly, "Oh no, of course, I asked her to be my maid of honor, I'd love for her to come!"

"I need to get a dress also, so Jenny, you can help me pick out one too," Susan said.

"Maybe I could find a dress for me too," Brenda added as well.

"Wow," James teased, "That's a big day out for the girls. Hurry hide your wallet, Sam."

Everyone started laughing.

"Hey, mom," Jenny said, "I'm planning on staying with red colors. Everything is already decorated in Christmas decor so that it will be easy on my budget and my time."

"Great choice," Sam said, "I love Christmas and all its decorations."

Susan invited Brenda to help her with the meal. She said she had planned a simple dinner and wanted all of them to get together to get to know each other. "No wedding talk tonight, just fun talk and relaxation."

"Us boys are going out fishing tomorrow," Sam informed everyone else that was present.

Matt and James seemed to be happy to hear that.

The following morning, the smell of coffee and bacon seemed to wake everyone up slowly, one at a time.

"Mom," Jenny said, "What a spread."

"Anything for you and your new family," Susan giggled.

"That sounds so nice," she added. Jenny hugged her mom and told her how much she loved her. Then she proceeded to kiss both her hands to acknowledge all that she had done for her.

Susan was dancing around in excitement, saying, "We get to go see dresses today. I'm your mom, and we get to fuss over you today. I know you don't like being the center of attention, but you can deal with it today. Have you thought about what style of dress you'd like?" Susan was over the moon. She couldn't contain her excitement for a split second. She kept thinking about the wedding, and couldn't wait to see her little girl dressed as a bride.

"Yes," Jenny answered, "I love lace, but I'd like to see
if there was a dress with a hood. I don't want tight-fitting
or a ball gown. I want to be comfortable enough to enjoy
the day."

Susan started pretending to walk like a model.
"Look, baby girl, I'm on the runway," Susan joked.

They began to laugh together. Jenny was still trying
to describe the dress idea between the laughter when
Brenda and Matt walked into the kitchen.

Matt asked with a sarcastic voice, "And what are we
missing out on?"

"Well," Brenda shouted, and she joined Susan for the
model walk, and they all started laughing and pointing to
Susan and Brenda.

Everyone got their food and sat at the breakfast
nook, built into a bay window overlooking the pool. James
was just getting out of the pool with Sam.

Susan said, "They went for an early morning swim."
It seemed like they were already getting along quite well.

The two walked in and got breakfast, and joined the rest to eat. Jenny told them they had booked Giovanni's Restaurant.

"Yes," James said, "We plan to do an Italian variety dish, a trio. Lasagna, alfredo, and chicken parmesan with salad, and Italian bread."

"That sounds wonderful!" Susan was pleased.

It was family time, and the couple couldn't make time for each for obvious reasons. But they had this coming, and they had already discussed it. Still, James would somehow try to catch Jenny's eye, and flirt with her casually every now and then. But they kept it subtle, especially when everyone was around. They just wanted to make sure that both their families felt included in the wedding.

As everyone was gathered around the breakfast table, there was a knock at the door.

"I'm here," a soft voice said as they door flew open. Jenny ran to the door instantly knowing who it was. She was squealing in excitement. She came back into the room with a beautiful, tall, curly-headed blonde with big blue eyes.

"This is my cousin Debrah," she introduced her to everyone.

"Oh, Deb, thanks for coming. I was so happy you agreed to be my maid of honor. I'm getting married," Jenny was jumping in excitement.

"Yes, yes, I am excited and honored to do it," Deb replied.

The two girls walked to the other room to talk for a minute.

Susan said, "Let's just take our plates to the sink. I have someone cleaning up for us today. I wanted us all just to enjoy being together."

A few minutes later, the girls came back into the room.

Susan announced, "It's time for us ladies to go. We don't want to be late for our appointments."

While Sam said, "With our fishing trip today, maybe we'll catch dinner for tonight."

Jenny and James hugged and kissed, "I will miss you terribly," they said to each other as they knew they would be spending time away for the day.

The girls ran out the door, and the guys decided to head out after about an hour.

"We'll be going out on the boat," Sam told them and asked if that was ok.

Matt and James both agreed with much enthusiasm.

Sam said, "The boat is only about a ten-minute drive. My friend Kenny will be going with us to be our boat captain for the day so that we can spend time together having fun."

Sam pulled out a map and showed James and Matt the planned trip.

"We'll travel out on the Saint Johns river straight to the ocean, and we can travel out a few miles to catch the good fish. Red snapper is the most plentiful and is always a good meal."

Matt shouted, "Wow! This will be our first time out on the ocean fishing."

"I bet we'll have as much fun as the girls," James declared.

He grabbed his camera on his way out the door and said, "Dad, we'll need proof to show everyone. I plan to catch the biggest one to impress Jenny."

Matt just laughed and said to Sam, "Do you hear that?"

They got to the boat.

"Wow!" That was what you could hear Matt and James saying as they walked to the yacht. Both of their jaws dropped open. It was a beautiful boat, and the day was even more suitable for fishing.

The boat was a pretty good-sized fishing boat, with all the poles, canopy, and cool chairs to fish from. Everyone sat down, and Kenny came out from down below. Sam introduced him to everyone as he pulled in the dock ropes, and they pulled away.

"If either of you gets queasy, let me know. There is a bathroom and beds to lay down on the lower level, and the life jackets are hanging here."

James stood alongside and looked out over the edge.

It took about forty minutes to get to where they wanted.

"Time to fish," Sam smiled. He was really looking forward to this day, and it had finally arrived.

Matt was first to get his pole in the water. Kenny put on some music, and Sam cracked open the sodas for everyone. James got the first bite after a short while as Sam helped him bring it in. It wasn't the biggest catch of the day, but it was the first.

Matt sarcastically remarked, "Well, that's not much bigger than a goldfish. Be sure to get that one on camera. Jenny will be so impressed." They all laughed. The boys called it a day after three hours on the water.

James asked if he could swim in the pool after they got back. Matt offered to help clean the fish and get it ready for the evening meal.

James offered to help to cook as well, "I love to cook for Jenny."

While out on the boat, they learned so much about each other as they kept the conversation going on. They caught seven fish together. Matt caught more than just fish. He also got a pretty good sunburn on the top of his balding head.

"Oh, Dad, James said you forgot your hat." All three of them started laughing.

They knew how much that would hurt later. James said, "You'll milk that one for a while, and mom will fall for it. She always does."

Matt and Sam decided to stay in the house, and James headed out for the pool. Both fathers had shared their love for their families, and they both spoke about their jobs. Matt was a shorter and stout man.

"James had not gotten that gene from me," Matt said with a chuckle. "James is tall, my other son Jack is shorter like me, but we all have red hair. Both boys got their looks from their mother."

Sam was a very tall man, six foot one. "I have to be honest. Jenny got her looks, those dark hair, and eyes from her birth mom. She died shortly after Jenny was born.

Susan and I met at church about a year later, and we got married. Jenny instantly became hers. Susan treats her as her own, and so much love has grown between those two. You would never know."

"Jenny never told us," Matt said. "That is so wonderful."

Sam's hair was dark but had a lot of grays. For anyone who had good observation could tell. However, the bonding Susan and Jenny shared was nothing less than what a mother and her daughter have.

"Fish tonight, but tomorrow we're going for the best crab in town. The dockside cafe'. They make the very best crab cake," Sam boasted.

The door flew open, and it was their girls back from their shopping trip. They were shouting and laughing and dancing all around and making memories and swapping stories; their shopping was done, and they told the men all about it!

CHAPTER FOUR

The girls got to the bridal shop. Jenny walked directly to the area of red dresses on the other side of the shop. It was an entire wall, and it looked like a rainbow. Every color and shade you could think of was present in the room.

Deb, being the maid of honor, joined her too, "Jenny, there are so many shades of red."

"Yes, I agree, I didn't even know those existed," Jenny chuckled.

Susan was busy checking in at the front desk. Brenda walked up behind Jenny and whispered in her ear, "I'll match the flowers to any color you pick." "Oh, thank you," Jenny said as she turned and hugged Brenda.

Cousin Deb asked, "What length and style of dress do you want me to wear?"

"Wear what makes you happy and comfortable. Find something you can always wear again." Jenny was being reasonable. She didn't want to put her cousin in a tough spot by demanding too much. However, she added that her favorite were the darker shades.

Deb pulled out a tea-length lace-off-the-shoulder A-line dress with short sleeves.

"Oh, Jenny, look, I love this," she gasped.

"So do I," Jenny said as she walked over to it. Deb said, "It's burgundy; maybe they can get it in red on time."

"Oh no," Jenny said, "It's perfect, with your blonde hair. You will look terrific."

Deb squealed like a little girl, "I want to try it on!"

A lady walked over and introduced herself, "I'm Miss Kate, this is my shop, and I'll be assisting you today."

"Hello, I'm Deb, cousin and maid of honor to the bride. Thank you, I'd like to try this one, please."

She took Deb to the dressing room. A few minutes later, Deb came out of the dressing room twirling and dancing. She truly looked happy.

"I believe this is it," she shouted.

"Wow! I can't imagine you in anything else," Jenny said.

"It fits me so perfectly, it's comfortable, and I love it. I'll take it!" Deb shouted.

Then she yelled across the room. "Hey Aunt Susan, hurry, you're missing this! I got my dress already!" Susan walked up to Jenny and put her arms around her, "It's beautiful, and it's perfect. This dress was made for her," she said.

"Deb, you're lucky to be Jenny's maid of honor," Susan added again jokingly.

Susan pointed to another area in the store and told Brenda, "That's where they have our dresses. We'll get ours picked out last."

Brenda grinned and said, "Wonderful, this place is amazing."

Deb went back into the dressing room. Miss Kate told them that the room was ready for the bride. The girls started making their way to the other side of the store.

They really couldn't wait to see Jenny try one of the bridal dresses for the very first time.

Deb ran to catch up with them, all while holding on to her dress.

Another young girl walked over and introduced herself. "I'm Hilary, and I'll be assisting Miss Kate today. There is a table here with tea, coffee, water, and cookies. Please help yourself," she said in a polite tone.

All the staff present was extremely careful and professional. She took Debbie's dress from her hands to assist her to get a dress form. By placing Debbie's dress next to the wedding dress, Jenny was now able to see how they would look together.

Jenny told Miss Kate when the wedding was and where they were planning to celebrate their day. Miss Kate asked Jenny, "What exactly are you looking for, and have you tried any dresses on already?" Jenny replied, "No, I have not tried anything on yet. I think I might like a dress with a hood because it is winter." Miss Kate asked, "Would you consider a hooded cape to wear over your dress?"

"Maybe, that might be nice too," Jenny answered. "I have two hooded dresses in the shop. We will pull them for you. Please don't limit yourself to only a couple of dress designs that have hoods. We have a great variety of other styles for you to look at as well." Miss Kate said politely. Jenny told her she understood. She then began to describe what else she liked. "I like lace-off white or ivory. I also like A-line and nothing tight-fitting. I want to enjoy my day, laugh, and eat!" Jenny laughed. "I understand. Well, let's try on dresses." Miss Kate chuckled. She then recommended the first dress be similar to the bridesmaid dress. It's an ivory and lace A-line, with satin trim at the top that goes off the shoulder, no sleeves, and a medium-length train. Jenny said, "Ok, I'm ready," and they walked over to the dressing room. Hilary went to get two more dresses that fitted Jenny's description. One dress was white with beading and pearls. It looked just like the bridesmaid dress, except that it had beads and

pearls. While the other was a hooded candlelight stretch satin, it was really soft. She brought them to the dressing room, and a happy scream came from behind the door. Susan said, "Now I'm excited!" Brenda started to cry, "Me too!" she said. Jenny walked out and stepped up on the platform. Mirrors were wrapping around half of her. Jenny could see herself entirely for the first time and in front of her family. The dress was a perfect fit and looked beautiful on her. Jenny was crying. "I love it!" She said, "I do want to try on the other dresses as well. The white dress has caught my attention, it's a little more sparkly than what I would normally wear, but it's beautiful. I wanted to save for last." Back she went to the dressing room.

Jenny tried the candlelight hooded dress next. "I like it," she said, "But it's not the one. It has too much fitting." She went out to show her family, they all agreed with her, it did look beautiful on her. Brenda told Jenny she would look stunning in anything she would wear. Jenny hurried to the dressing room to try on the last dress; although white, Jenny loved it on the hanger.

While the dress was being zipped up and buttoned, she started to cry. She put her hands to both sides of her face and shouted, "Wow, oh my gosh, I want this dress, I love it!" Her reaction said it all.

She went out to the platform, and the girls stood up, and to their surprise, Jenny was wearing her summer sundress. "This is a total shocker! Wow!" Susan said.

Brenda and Deb were crying and laughing at the same time as they hugged each other.

Miss Kate said, "The dress chosen does come in ivory."

Jenny said, "No, I love the white." Hillary then brought the white winter hooded cape. It was a very soft satin, and it went perfect with the dress.

Jenny told Miss Kate, "I don't even need the cape. I love my dress and don't want to cover it up."

Miss Kate asked, "What about a veil then?' Jenny told her, "I am planning to wear Christmas flowers in my hair."

Miss Kate smiled and nodded.

"Mom, you aren't too upset with me for keeping the dress a total surprise? Are you?" Jenny asked.

"No, I love the idea of seeing you for the first time with your dad on your wedding day. You know that will make me cry again." Susan said.

They hugged again for the hundredth time that day. Hilary was sure to bring the bridesmaid dress into the dressing room so Jenny could see the dresses next to each other. Jenny returned to the dressing room with Miss Kate to look at the dresses. They were so perfect together and were syncing in the most amazing way. Miss Kate took Jenny's hand and told her how special she thought keeping the surprise for everyone was. She showed Jenny how the buttons went so Deb could help her get dressed.

Hillary took the mothers to the area of the shop for the selection of dresses for them. Brenda found a beautiful lace dress that looked great on her, and Susan found a tea-length dress that fitted her perfectly. Jenny was so excited that they all had found dresses. Both the mothers found the perfect burgundy dresses. Jenny said, "We all will be beautiful." Brenda remembered she had a white fur shawl, "It belonged to James' grandmother," she said. "May we check it out, back in Chicago?"

Jenny asked. "Yes, yes you may," said Brenda with much enthusiasm, "She'll be so excited to see you in it."

Miss Kate took them to the adjoining shop. "They have shoes here; you may find something you want, or something might catch your eye," she said with a smile. Jenny's dark eyes turned into bright open pools.

"Wow!" Susan said. Jenny quickly made her way to the white shoes, which lined the back and sidewalls. She found a pair that had some lace and a few pearls on them.

"Mom," she shouted. "Look, these will work well with my dress, and they're pumps!"

"Oh Jenny, my darling!" Susan said, "They are absolutely perfect!" Jenny asked the clerk for her size. "I sure hope they are comfortable, mom," Jenny said.

"I hope they are too, baby girl," mom replied. Miss Kate came in with the color number for each of the dresses. Roman walked over and introduced himself. He was the owner. He dyed and decorated the shoes to order. He was also Miss Kate's brother. Brenda commented, "That is a lost art and a rare find. Can you dye the shoes to match a swatch?" Brenda asked.

Roman said, "Yes, as long as it is my shoes, I'm able to use sample fabric to test with."

"That makes sense," Brenda said. "I have a suit at home. I would love shoes to match. Can I purchase them today and mail you a swatch of fabric?"

"Yes," Roman answered.

"Great!" She said, "I would like to try these on."

Deb found the shoes with lace only that would match her dress perfectly. The girls were so happy with their shopping day.

"Mom," Jenny asked, "Did I go over the budget today? I never even asked you."

"No way, my dear," Susan replied.

Susan said, "Let's go for ice cream." While having ice cream, Brenda asked Susan if there was a particular jewelry store she liked. She said, "I want to get Jenny a necklace to wear for the wedding."

Jenny overheard and said, "Awh, how sweet, my something new."

"This is from Matt's mom, grandma Gertie. She's the one in the nursing home; this is a gift from her." Susan said, "I know the place; let's go."

They walked into Barton's Jewelers. It had been around for seventy-five years. Brenda asked, "Could we find something with pearls or little diamonds to match your dress?"

"Yes," Jenny said, "Whatever you think grandma would like." Brenda headed to the counter where the pearl jewelry was. There she saw an open heart necklace made of pearls as a border.

"Oh, Jenny," she said, "Look at this!" "It's so explicitly beautiful!" Jenny awed.

Brenda also saw an open heart with a single pearl at the bottom. Jenny said, "Oh, this one is nice."

Cousin Deb looked over and said, "That one is so you, the single pearl in the heart."

Jenny asked Brenda, "Which one do you like the best?" Jenny continued to add, "I would be happy with any of them and honored to wear whatever you pick for me."

Brenda saw another open heart with two small diamonds along the side, "I think this one is the one I would pick for you. One heart and two diamonds each for you and James," she said.

"Oh yes. Thank you. It's perfect, and I love it. I want to wear it now and always." Jenny agreed wholeheartedly.

CHAPTER FIVE

A knock at the door startled James. It was the secretary with the mail. The morning was gone, and the afternoon had just begun. He knew he had to do some work today, but he couldn't get it past his heart. James by no means was a procrastinator, but today he just could not function. He picked up an Anniversary card lying on his desk. It was a beautiful card intricately embellished with gold raised lettering and a single long stem rose attached with gold embossed on the front. He ran his fingers over the lettering, "Happy Anniversary." "I love you," was inscribed on the card.

After a sad, slow deep breath, he said, "Please, come back to me, Jenny." He opened the card and picked up his pen. He began writing.

You are the love of my life. You have been since day one.

And you will be until our day is done.

Those were the words he said in his wedding vows to Jenny the day they were married. He continued to write.

You are my best friend to the end.

I love you

James

He put his pen down and looked at his wedding ring, he rubbed his finger over it, and his eyes filled with tears. "Oh Jenny, what do we do?" James cried out, having left no restraint on his emotions. He wiped his eyes and stopped to stare out the window again. The mountains were snow-covered, and the sight was breathtaking. Again he drifted away. It was their wedding day. The campus church was decorated beautifully with clear twinkle lights. A wonderful Christmas tree was in the front corner of the church with white ornaments and a crystal star on top.

White poinsettias were placed in each window and across the front of the church. It looked magical, all dreamy and hazy.

James and Jack walked to the front of the church with the pastor. As he turned to look out at his family, he saw his mom and dad. His mom stood up and went up to hug and kiss James. She said, "I love you," and turned to walk back to her place next to dad.

James' grandmother from the nursing home was sitting next to his dad. James stepped down and walked over to her, enclosing her in a big hug. He stopped in front of his dad and shook hands. James pulled his dad close and put an arm around his dad for a hug. "Thank you, dad," he said. He leaned over and hugged his mom again. James went back to his place at the altar.

The music started to play, and the large doors opened in a dramatic manner, or so it seemed. Everyone stood and turned around to see the bride. Debbie stepped through, and Jack tapped James on the shoulder and said, "Look, she's gonna be my girl." Debbie grinned and winked at Jack. He smiled back and stiffened up like a proud man. Jenny then took her place in the center of the doors alone for just a quick moment. She looked like an angel, nothing less than that. It felt as if time stood still, and there was no one else in the church but just the two of them.

A flush of emotions filled James, and he began to cry. Jenny's mom and dad stepped into the doorway, taking their place. Her mom took hold of her left arm, and dad took her right arm. Jenny chose not to carry flowers. Instead, she decided to hold her mom's arm. They stopped at the pew for the parents, and Jenny's mom kissed her and said, "I love you," and took her place. Jenny and her dad resumed their walk to the altar. All the time, she kept her eyes on James. When they stopped, the pastor asked, "Who would give this woman to be married to this man?"

Dad replied, "Her mother and I do." But just then, from the group of friends in the pews, you could hear them say, "We do too." A wave of laughter consumed the entire church at for the moment. Jenny's dad placed her hand in James' hand, "Take good care of her," he said, and then he turned around and walked away. Jenny and James watched him take his seat as he hugged his wife. "My daddy's crying," she said quietly.

Jenny and James looked into each other's eyes, and they both had tears; James grinned and said, "You look like an angel, my angel." Jenny said with all the love radiating from her eyes. "Thank you, and someone's looking nice too." They both took deep breaths and tightened up their grips on each other's hands. The pastor said, "Jenny and James have written their vows." Jenny began hers first and then James. They exchanged rings and cried through it all. The next thing said was, "You may kiss your wife." They kissed and hugged through the tears as the guests began to cheer. It was a moment of pure love. The big announcement came. The pastor introduced them. "It is my pleasure to introduce, for the first time, "Mr. and Mrs. James Lucks." There was more applause and cheering from the guests as they stepped down from the altar and stopped to greet their parents. Then the two of them went out to the front of the chapel to greet every guest. Debbie and Jack were holding hands. Debbie's parents Aunt Dottie and Uncle Buck had come from Florida just for the wedding. Jenny was so delighted to see them. Roberto, who was the last in line, was full of hugs and spoke mostly in Italian. He then yelled out, "E l'ora di mangiare! Time to eat! Celebrazione! Noi Andiamo! We go to Giovanni's!" he yelled. Roberto hurried on his way.

They arrived at the restaurant, and everyone was there to greet them. The room was decorated to the level of perfection, just the way Jenny wanted. Small flower arrangements were at each place, setting as a keepsake. They looked like little gift boxes filled with baby poinsettias and tiny white roses, and the lids tilted off to one side. Little paper sleighs filled with candies were also placed at each place setting. She went to her mother and mother-in-law and thanked them. "It was all really beautiful," she told them. Jenny's mom told her Aunt Dottie had helped also. Jenny made sure to let her aunt know how much she appreciated her for helping her out with the decoration part.

Roberto had surprised them with an *hors-d'oeuvre* *t*able with all kinds of treats to taste. The cake was on a round table in the corner with a light shining as it sparkled. The cake was simple but sheerly elegant, with white icing and clear sanding crystals and snowflakes.

A beautiful crystal snowflake with their names engraved on it was placed on the top. The cake itself was an Italian rum cake. The lights dimmed, and the announcement was made that the dinner would be served in thirty-five minutes. Most of their thirty guests were enjoying the *hors d'oeuvre* table and just visiting each other. The waiter brought the Italian bread to the table. It was hot with an aroma that drew people to their seats, and salads were brought out. James' brother started with the toasting for the bride and groom. The last glass was filled with wine, and they all raised a glass to Jenny and James.

Everyone was enjoying the food and conversation. Mostly all plates were empty, and everyone raved about how great the food was and how full they had been. Roberto put on the music and told everyone to dance. "Ballo, ballo, dance, dance!" he said. Jenny and James got up and danced together for their first dance. Then the guests joined them. The professor from the theatrical class and his wife were dancing like school kids, and some of their classmates had come as well. "Love is in the air! L'amore e nell'aria!" Roberto exclaimed with awe as he walked into the room. He had a gift for the newlyweds. He paid one hundred dollars toward the reception dinner, a total surprise. Jenny and James thanked him with numerous hugs and kisses.

Uncle Buck walked up to James and Jenny and handed them an envelope. "Open it," he said. "Hurry, hurry!" He insisted as he shook his fists in excitement. He couldn't wait; he just blurted it out, "You leave Monday for Vail Colorado for a ski resort honeymoon!" Aunt Dottie said, "We know it's your favorite thing to do."

"Wow! Wow!" Jenny and James said at the same time, and they were so excited and overwhelmed at the same time. "I had not made any plans for us to go anywhere. Thank You so much, really!" They hugged. James' parents told them there was a trust fund set aside to buy a house. Jenny's parents had bought them a car for graduation and paid for the reception. The two were overwhelmed with the gifts they had received from their families.

Jenny stopped and took a moment to go to James' grandmother, to thank her again for the necklace. Jenny showed her that she was wearing it. Jenny told Gertie she loved it and would always wear it. Jenny also thanked her for the use of her white shawl. Grandma Gertie told them she owned two houses in Colorado. One was for James, and one was for Jack. She told them they could either live in them or sell them. It was their choice.

Jack took James aside and said, "We should go into the business together; there is an idea I have. I'll explain it all when you get home from Vail."

Debbie decided to stay a couple more weeks in Chicago. James' parents invited her to stay with them. Jack was very happy to have her stay.

CHAPTER SIX

When James and Jenny returned home from Vail, Debbie told them that she was moving to be close to Jack. Jack proclaimed his love for Debbie, and they were over the moon. James and Jenny were very happy for them, and they wanted Jack and Debbie to progress together in love. Jack sat with them and told him about the business idea that he had earlier discussed. It was to start their own publishing company. It would be risky, but he knew they could do it with a down payment from all parties.

"We would move to Colorado where grandma has given us houses, and we live in them. No mortgages. All three sets of parents were on board."

James said, "You've been busy while we were gone." Jack told them he was prepared. James said, "We need to do more research."

Jack shared that he and Debbie had already started searching for various buildings. She showed them she had already found two buildings. Both properties are a short commute to the houses. The properties were reasonably priced.

James and Jenny looked at each other, and both agreed, it was worth looking into. They decided they would go together and take a look, right after Christmas. Jack pulled up the business numbers and the demographics. It was as if he had prepared for this all his life.

James sat at the computer, amazed by his brother. Jack said, "We need to put our college education to work. Jenny, you love to read and write, and James, you edit very well, and you plan to own a business. Debbie is on the financial side, and I was a business major. We have a team to make this work. We should plan to go two days after Christmas; Jenny's parents will meet us there." Debbie's dad "Buck" is coming with Jenny's parents. James' parents were also going. Jack said, "The entire family is on board, and we have to make this work." Jack made up a business plan and a full itinerary for the trip. Jack was more than excited, and he wanted to pursue this business idea.

Two days after Christmas, they opened up grandma's houses, so they had places to stay. The following day the whole family was there.

As the business idea proceeded, a meeting was scheduled the following afternoon, and the real estate agent had found them six properties to look at. She was a boss-lady for a full-proof plan, and then she scheduled three properties to visit each day.

As they were done with inspecting all the properties, everyone was in favor of two properties. The parents were all on board to help with the investment. Family and business partners, Jack had all the numbers crunched. They all finally choose the property with extra square footage for future expansion or rental space opportunities.

It was just outside the city but close to the main road. Jack pulled up the business plan to share with everyone. Debbie and James had researched all the equipment needed to start this business up. Everything was proceeding just like a business plan between professional partners. The building would not be available until March first. All parents agreed to take a thirty-day vacation to help fix up the building.

They all sat down that night and decided what they could do and what work they needed a construction company to do. They all threw names around, but in the end, Jenny had the best idea. "We are in an old town," she said, "Why not call it "Ole Towne Publishing." Jack said, "Let me get our name out there and see if we get authors." That night became the foundation of their publishing business, and after considering the feasibility plan for the projected business, everyone went home.

There was a lot on their plates; therefore, Jack and James promptly applied for the permits and business licenses required to start a business. They even hired a construction company and crew to get the business progress easily.

Time passed quickly. It was the end of February, and they were all finished moving into the houses. On the 28th of the same month, everyone was gathered, where Debbie and Jack announced their engagement. Everyone was more than happy with the announcement because it was the most expected thing to experience. Debbie and Jack were fiercely in love and were looking into each other's eyes deeply. Love was in the air, and it was the sweetest thing to witness.

Exactly two months after the engagement, they got married in a private family gathering. Everyone liked the couple as they looked beautiful together.

Meanwhile, Jack had received several author inquiries. Debbie found an established writer for children's books, and he was willing to give them a shot. After putting in their utmost efforts, they opened the doors officially for their business. It was just in three months, June 1st, that they were able to proceed with different business procedures on official terms. A grand opening for their business happened as they all were quite keen to take part in this newly born business individually.

Six months after the grand opening, Jenny found out that she and James were having a baby. It was the happiest moment in their lives, and they could not think of any better future but to raise their child in the best ways possible.

As far as the progress of business was concerned, it grew tremendously in the next six months. They were able to expand into all books. Jenny was even writing children's books, and James was editing them. They hired an artist to do all the graphics. It was something they were cherishing each passing day and somehow making memories for their loving child.

CHAPTER SEVEN

Months went by, and the day came when the entire family was there at the hospital in June when Toby was born. He was the first grandchild for both families. Jenny and James felt like proud parents because they could sense smiles and blessings everywhere in the hallway.

Jenny and James's families stayed a couple of days after Toby came home from the hospital. The grandmas held him almost all day long. It was becoming their favorite thing to do, taking care of their baby grandson. They loved being there to help in any way possible. They pampered him danced with him, sang to him, and just loved him fully.

Alone for the first time as parents Jenny and James began to adjust to the new routine. About a week after Toby came home, he stopped eating, and dark spots appeared on his body. Jenny could not believe her eyes. She panicked, and they rushed little Toby to the doctor. The doctor admitted Toby to the hospital for observation and testing.

Jenny and James stayed at the hospital by Toby's side. It seemed so unfair for a little one to be kept in the hospital, hooked up to so many machines instead of being in the love and warmth of his home.

All James and Jenny could do were to wait. They pondered on the worst possibilities but prayed and hoped for the best during this challenging time.

All Jenny seemed to do was cry and hold Toby's little hands. "I love you, baby boy," she would say to him often. She remembered how happy they were on his arrival and wished they could go back in time to help him sooner. James kept telling Toby he was sorry and that he would trade places with him if it were possible. After three days of testing was over, growths began to appear on little Toby's skull.

The doctors were aware that the parents were not ready for the results of testing, especially if it was negative. The next morning two doctors came in to see Jenny and James in Toby's room. They had to deliver the sad news that little Toby had stage four brain cancer – a rare and untreatable disease. They were in shock, and they were so numb that they couldn't speak a word. They couldn't even ask any questions. The doctors left them alone for about an hour to be with Toby and to absorb the information they had received. One doctor returned to answer any questions the couple might have.

James asked only one. Not how long did Toby have? But how long do we have together? The doctor said that he only had a few days. Jenny gasped and asked whether they could take him home to be with the family.

The doctor was also crying and said, Yes. Toby will be ready to go home in an hour.

That was the longest hour They had ever experienced. James made the calls to all the family. Everyone dropped everything and returned to Colorado. Debbie and Jack were at the house to help them when they arrived home.

Jenny and James spent the next three days holding little Toby, even when the hospice nurse administered his pain medication. They never let go of his hands and always made sure they told him about their love for him and what a good boy he had been. Toby died after three days of pure love pouring out from all the family members.

Their pain was so great that they remained home alone for the next month. They sat at his gravesite for hours and cried together. The pain of losing a child can never go away. When two people conceive together, they start knitting various dreams for their child. They get deeply moved with the addition in their lives. The comfort and peace of their child become their only consideration in their lives. Jenny and James were going through that dreadful part of their lives that no one could imagine feeling their pain.

For their support, Jenny's mom stayed a few days, she tried to cook meals, but both refused to eat. They were not in their senses, and they wanted to get back to their son and save him from dying due to a fatal disease.

Jenny's mother was there, and she always offered to help in any way she could, but they didn't take anyone's help. After a month, they both went back to work. Jenny went home early most days. James would come home and find her sitting in his bedroom crying. James had tried to be the strong one, but he often found himself staring out his office window or walking in the park alone crying. They both visited the cemetery but never together anymore.

Jenny stopped writing, the thing she loved the most. She and James stopped living and rarely spoke to each other for the next year and a half. They buried themselves in their work. They stopped hanging out with friends or family. They were the happy couple who was always there for others, but it was a difficult time for them and had changed the way they used to be.

They had a new baby niece they never visited; they just couldn't; the loss of their newborn was not old yet, and they were unable to look beyond the death of their son.

It hurt too bad. They didn't celebrate holidays or birthdays. Four months after Toby's death, they had closed up his bedroom and never went into it again. There was no talk of Toby or their feelings. Neither one was unkind or spoke a harsh word. Jenny stopped laughing and never smiled anymore. James didn't know what to do, to help.

They didn't take any days off from work. Their families had become very concerned, but they never took anyone's advice. James knew they had to do something, as they had been this way for eighteen months.

There was a knock on the door again; it was Jack. He walked in, saying, "I see you out there, brother." Jack told James he was working on the end of the year reports. "Do you need to review them before I finalize the year," he asked.

"No, you've always done it perfectly. I'm positive it won't need my attention," replied James.

"James," Jack said, "Go, go away for a few days. I can handle things here for as long as you need. You need some time off."

"Thank you," James said.

Jack told James, "You might be my little brother, but it's been almost two years. It's time to do something. Okay, I'm out of here," Jack said. "Deb and I are going to lunch. I'll check back in when we get back."

James replied, "Have a nice time and please close the door on your way out; thanks again."

He turned to his computer and started looking at a getaway place.

CHAPTER EIGHT

The next day, James took an unexpected afternoon off from work. It has been ages that he had taken any off, for a vacation or even for sickness. He picked Jenny up after work, and when they got home, he told her he had decided they needed to go away. Jenny was clueless about the fact, and she was trying to process it all through her mind.

Jenny stood stunned for a moment. He told her he had planned an entire trip the week before Christmas and the week after. It was a business shutdown time, so there was no reason they couldn't go. There was a spark in James' eyes and a hope that maybe Jenny would agree with the plan.

She then started making all kinds of excuses for why they couldn't go. "No, Jenny," James said. He then asked in a stern voice, "Why, why Jenny, what is the real reason, why can't we leave?" She didn't answer. She couldn't answer. Jenny just stood there speechless and cried. James said, "I give you one reason we need to go, and it is to save us. We are worth that. You see, we have stopped living. My love, all these months, we are only surviving, and for what? We don't even know that. We have not talked to each other, and it's been a great deal of time."

As he approached her, she backed away. James couldn't even get close enough to console her crying. He told her he couldn't go on like this anymore; this might be their last chance. James also explained before she could accuse him, it wasn't another woman. She was the only woman he loved and would ever love, and they needed fixing. James continued, "We are married because we decided to go through everything together, no matter how much good or bad it would be, we promised to hold each other hands tightly in the moment of distress and happiness."

It was not something new to Jenny, and thus she agreed they needed to do something to mend their marriage. She told him that she loved him but felt so empty inside that it wasn't his fault. James said, "We never speak of him, and I'm empty also. I miss him too."

James pulled his fist to his chest and then pointed down the hallway to Toby's bedroom door. We've never moved on, and neither of us goes into his room, the door always stays shut, and we never mention his name. I haven't been to his grave in three months. I'm not proud of my actions, but Toby was our son together. James pointed his finger at Jenny and then to himself when he told her. "We were a family for however long it was. I want to have a chance again, together. If we will not communicate it now, we will never be able to move on in our lives," he added.

"I love you for better or for worse. It's time to work for better." Jenny continued crying, and she leaned up against a wall to support her. James took a deep breath and stepped away for a second. He was fighting back his emotions after he had just put it all out there for her.

He turned back and told her where they were going. "The Blue Spruce Spa," up in the mountains of Colorado. A resort whose specialty is a couples retreat.

Everything was for couples only, massages, saunas, private dinners, skiing, and snowboarding time. There was even a couple's counselor on staff. James felt this was the first step and Jenny agreed to try. "We both need this, and you know I'm right," James said.

He told her they would leave in two days, and they were not backing out. He walked away and went to the bedroom so he could cry in private. He was relieved a bit because it was the first time since Toby died that he had a heart-to-heart conversation with the love of his life.

The following two days, Jenny put stuff in her suitcase and then talked herself into not going and then putting her clothes away. She was beginning to stress herself out over the trip. It was not at all easy for her. The night before they were to leave, James looked at Jenny's suitcase; it was empty.

"I guess you're not wearing any clothes on this trip," he sarcastically said.

"Well, maybe I should dress the same way." Jenny annoyingly looked at James and took a deep breath, and packed some clothes.

The following day, Jenny explained last-minute details to the managing editor and needed to wait to leave until her work was done.

Jenny had been on the phone for a very long time with the editor for the last-minute details. Most of the staff would be on a business shut down with full pay for two weeks starting at five pm. They were very generous to their team.

It was a six-hour drive to the "The Blue Spruce Spa," and it was getting late in the afternoon. James came in from packing the car and, with a firm voice, told Jenny, "We need to get on the road now. We have to drive through the mountains, so let's go."

Jenny got in the car and looked so scared. James held her hand tightly and told her to relax. Jenny started texting the manager after about ten minutes into the start of the trip. She talked to her phone like it was a person in front of her. James never spoke a word. He just listened and let her have the time she needed, and it seemed to calm her. After all, it was about the business.

Three hours had passed, and it started snowing. Neither one thought anything about it. Light snow in the mountains was in the forecast. Jenny was finishing conducting her business. It had been about another half hour. Jenny looked up and saw it snowing more heavily and ended her business call quickly, ensuring she relayed a Merry Christmas to all from her and James. It was 04:30 pm; therefore, everyone was getting ready to go home.

"What's going on with the weather?" Jenny asked. James told her he wasn't sure, "A storm like this wasn't predicted or shown on the weather map."

He told her he had checked every report; light snow in the mountains was all that was in the forecast. Jenny started checking the weather report on her phone. It was only showing up as light snow and no wind. Very rapidly, the snow seemed to be getting very heavy, and it was getting dark. The wind continued getting worse. The radio wasn't even reporting a storm like this. They were only talking about two inches.

James said, "Yeah, two inches, more like we've had almost six inches in the last half hour. I'm glad we have four-wheel drive."

James started having trouble seeing the road. The wipers were not keeping the same pace as the snowfall. Jenny said, "We need to stop somewhere. We can't travel through this."

"There is no place to stop or even to ask for help," James replied.

He slowed way down. There were no other cars on the road. Jenny began to worry if they had gotten off on the wrong road somehow. She saw a road sign, and James got real close so she could read it. The highway sign indicated the correct route. James yelled out, "Woah!"

Their car began to slide. Jenny closed her eyes and tensed up in her seat. James put his arm out in front of her for extra protection. It seemed like the car traveled a long distance before it came to a sudden stop.

"Are you ok?" He asked.

A very quiet and shaky yes came from Jenny. James checked his phone for cell service.

"Perfect," he shouted out as he hit the steering wheel with both hands, "Nothing, no service!" He sat back in his seat, "I'm so sorry. I don't know; I just don't know," James said.

He tried a couple of times to back up and drive forward, but the car was stuck. Fearful of blaming her husband, Jenny stayed quiet for a couple of minutes. They had both agreed to be respectful of each other and try getting along.

She glanced up and saw something through his window. "Look," Jenny exclaimed! "There's a light over there. It's close," Jenny put her arm in front of him and pointed, "Maybe someone is there."

James replied, "I didn't see that light before; maybe the snow was blinding my view of it."

Jenny recommended they go and try to find help quickly because the storm seemed to be getting worse.

Without any second thought, they both got out of the car, the snow was deep, and their vehicle was stuck. James looked around to be sure they were off the road. He exclaimed, "There must be more than two feet of snow. This is crazy."

Jenny was having a hard time getting through the deep snow. James took her hand as they started walking together toward the light. It seemed like it was a mile walk through the wind that was piercing through their coats. The temperature seemed to be much colder than predicted. They could barely see their car, and it was only sixty feet away. They stopped, and in front of them was a well-lit log cabin. The snow on the steps and the porch looked like someone had shoveled it. Someone must be home.

James knocked on the door over and over each time, knocking louder. Jenny was yelling, "Hello, please help us!" She even tried tapping on the window. No one answered. The next knock on the door, Jenny helped out, and the door opened on its own.

James stepped back, and Jenny peeked her head in, asking, "Hello, is anyone here? Could you help us please?"

A big gust of wind hit James, and he fell into Jenny a little, which pushed her through the door; he then stepped in behind her. The door closed behind them on its own. It startled Jenny; she turned to run back out but bumped into James; they stood there staring into each other's eyes. It was a rare moment in all those months.

James felt awkward because they had not been that close to each other in such a long time and did not know what else to do; he backed up and said, "No one appears to be home, and their car is not here."

James commented, "This is like the first day we met snowing and blowing." Jenny grinned and turned away to look around. "I'm going to get our suitcases from the car. We can sit and wait until they come home," James said.

He opened the door and headed to the car. Jenny watched him through the window until she couldn't see him anymore, then she went to the door and waited. She heard footsteps on the porch and opened the door for him. She held the door open while he carried the luggage in. He was all covered with snow.

"Burrr!" James said as he started brushing off his snowy coat. Jenny helped him brush off some of the snow. Jenny had found a coat hook on the wall, "Here, let's hang our coats; your coat is wet," she said.

She turned and saw two substantial comfy chairs with a warm fire in the fireplace in the living room. The fire was tended to nicely, looking like someone had just made it. Jenny looked around and saw there was no television, no phone, and only an old radio.

"I don't see a phone anywhere in the cottage. We might not be able to get any help tonight. We still have no cell phone reception here either." she said.

"Oh boy," James sighed, "Looks like our vacation is off to a terrific start."

The kitchen was small, but there was an eat-in table and two chairs. James placed his head in his hands and put his elbows to the table. James sat down, "I believe I need a minute to get my thoughts together," he continued telling Jenny he didn't even see a shovel on the porch.

"Will we be stuck here all night?" Jenny questioned. "We're in a stranger's house! We can't stay here!" she shouted. She took a deep breath and began to cry.

While she was crying, she apologized, "I'm sorry, I didn't mean to panic. We hardly speak, and the last thing you need is for me to carry on. I've never raised my voice to you ever." James replied, "Maybe you're right. I've ruined our non-communication time." He continued after a deep breath. "I can't go on with our silent world, and we were going away to work through this. I'm not sure what comes next." Jenny walked away with tears in her eyes still.

She continued to check the rest of the cottage out. She found a bedroom with one bed and a bathroom with a shower and an old claw tub. Jenny dried her eyes, walked back to the kitchen, and told James what she had found.

They even saw a little area next to a window off the kitchen eating area. It had a little table and two chairs. "I wonder what this is for?" Jenny asked.

"Well," James said, "If they come home, maybe they'll let us camp out on the floor."

Jenny chuckled, "We haven't done that since college. I guess we could go sit by the fire and get warm."

"I'll try to get something on this old radio; maybe we can figure out our next move," James smiled and said.

Jenny chuckled sarcastically and said, "Yeah, like keeping us out of jail for breaking the law."

"Well, technically, the door opened on its own, the wind pushed us in the door, the door closed on its own. I guess, you could say we're prisoners," James said.

Jenny was watching James tuning the radio and heard a noise in the kitchen.

Jenny quickly ran to James and tapped his shoulder. "I heard it too," he whispered. He stood up, and they both strolled to the kitchen. Jenny flipped on the light switch.

James shouted, "Who's there?" No one answered. "Look, on the table, two cups," Jenny said as she peeked over at them.

"What just happened?" Jenny asked.

"This is two cups of hot tea. I'm also confused," James said, "But I believe I'm going to have a cup."

They both picked up a cup and checked it out carefully. "This is our favorite tea, and mine is sweetened just the way I like it," Jenny said.

"Mine too," said James, as he took a sip.

They walked back to the chairs in front of the fireplace. They heard another noise in the kitchen. Jenny got up and strolled to the kitchen. She found warm cookies on the table; Jenny looked around and didn't see anyone there. She picked up the plate, took it to the living room, and placed it on the coffee table between the chairs. "Wow, I was just thinking about cookies and food," James said and then added, "All I could get on the radio is some Christmas music."

Jenny said. "I'm scared. I wonder if we should go back to the car." James told her the car was buried in the snow, and they would freeze if they went out to sit in it.

"I think we have no choice but to stay and see what happens next; we appear to be safe here," James babbled on.

Jenny interrupted, "I get it."

It was getting very late.

Jenny asked, "Do you think we should use the bed?" James replied with a yawn, "Yes, we should."

They both headed into the bedroom. Jenny thought she might like to take a nice hot bath, and she asked James, "What do you think, should I?"

"Yes, we're here in someone's house getting ready to sleep in their bed. I guess a bath won't hurt; we can just add it to our arrest sheet," James laughed.

After her bath, Jenny looked out the window, only to see that the snow was not letting up. She could see the light hazy area where the moon should be. Jenny crawled into the bed and saw James, who was already asleep.

"We'll figure this out in the morning, and Lord, please keep us safe," she said under her breath.

CHAPTER NINE

The morning light slightly brightened the bedroom. Jenny awakened as she heard a noise coming from the kitchen. She grabbed James' arm, it startled him, and he woke up. Jenny put her finger to her mouth and motioned with her other hand to wait.

"There's a noise in the kitchen," she whispered. They both got up slowly and quietly, "I smell coffee, and it smells so good," James said.

"Shhh, walk quietly," She whispered.

"I smell cinnamon rolls too. It just fills the air; it's unbelievable. Maybe the owner is home." said James.

They both stood still, holding on to each other as they approached the kitchen. They managed to stretch their necks enough to peek around the corner. James couldn't take it any longer. He stepped out into the kitchen and looked around. No one was there. They were stunned to see two cups of hot coffee and a plate of fresh warm cinnamon rolls were on the table. The aroma was irresistible, and James was having a weak moment. "Well, I'm hungry," James said, "I know we don't eat like this normally but, I'm eating, have a seat with me."

He and Jenny sat at the table and ate. James told Jenny that the cinnamon rolls were as good as the ones from Marco's Bakery back in Chicago, and she agreed.

They were both baffled about everything. James, teasingly, said, "Maybe it's a ghost house, Jenny."

She jumped up and ran to the window and looked out, "That's not funny," Jenny yelled out!

"It's snowing worse than last night. It's gloomy out here, with no sun peeking through the clouds. I'm a little frightened," she said.

James replied, "I confess I'm a little leary too. Let's get dressed and we can go outside and check things out." Jenny responded, "I can barely see the car, look for yourself."

James walked past her and headed to the bedroom; Jenny followed. They were about half-dressed when they heard more noise coming from the living room, and it sounded like running water and dishes clanging together in the kitchen.

"What's going on?" Jenny whispered in a soft voice.

James ran out of the bedroom half dressed, yelling, "Who are you!"

No one was there, and the dishes were washed and put away.

"Ok, you have our attention. What's up?" he questioned out loud.

As he walked back to the bedroom, he noticed the fire was freshly tended to in the living room, and a Christmas tree was in the corner of the room. There were even a couple of bins.

"Ok, can someone please tell us what is going on in this house," he said even louder. Jenny came out of the bedroom, asking, "What's up?"

"Look, look," James shouted as he pointed to the living room. Jenny was stunned, and she stopped in her tracks.

"What's this?" she asked.

They both walked into the living room and looked at the tree, and then opened one of the bins, only to find lights and ornaments. James said, in a confused character voice, "This is unbelievable."

"There is an answer for this. Stop clowning around," Jenny said.

"Yeah, we just need to figure it out now," James demanded.

Jenny started to calm herself; she took a couple of deep breaths and decided to look around the kitchen. She saw dishes put away and everything cleaned up. She was getting curious about each thing and considering someone close to them doing all such things, just to amaze or tease them.

"Someone knows we're here, and I think they're helping us, quick James, finish getting dressed," Jenny said.

She went to the living room and sat down. James went to the bedroom to finish getting dressed. As he came out of the room, James asked, "What do you mean? Someone knows we're here, Jenny. Are you crazy?"

"Maybe I am. Do you have a better explanation?" she questioned.

"We have food to eat, coffee, a warm fire, and a place to sleep. We can't leave, our car is stuck, the snow is deep, there is no shovel, and it is still snowing," she said.

"What do you think?" she asked.

They were both getting overwhelmed. Jenny recommended they both relax.

"I guess we should decorate the tree. We aren't going anywhere today."

James replied and then babbled a bit, saying, "I just wish we could call the resort, so they don't cancel our reservation."

James sat in the other chair and took a deep breath, and sighed. "This is the most time we have spent together alone and the most we have spoken in a year and a half. Sadly, we are forced to do this rather than do it on our own. The main reason why I wanted us to go away together was to be together, so I guess we should make the best of our situation," he said.

Jenny started to cry, "I'm sorry, I haven't been able to talk about him. I'm just not ready. It hurts so bad, she sobbed.

"That's ok," James said, "You don't have to talk, there's no pressure, maybe we should try to decorate the tree; we didn't do that last year, maybe that will help us feel better."

James fidgeted with the radio again, and all he was still able to get was Christmas music. He left on the music, hoping to hear a weather report soon and still no cell phone service.

Meanwhile, Jenny wiped the tears and stopped crying. They started to decorate the tree when Jenny noticed something strange.

"They almost looked like our ornaments from home. That's weird," she said.

James took a close look and agreed, "It's not that weird from all that's happened up to this point, but you're right; this is exactly like the ornament I gave you on our first Christmas."

Jenny chuckled, "Let me see that up close. It is my ornament. Look! You put our first Christmas year on it. We didn't have a tree. We had just gotten married. This has to be a setup, but by whom, your parents, my parents, our best friends?" she questioned, "How could they have done this if we got stuck in the snow? How could they have gotten through? There are no tracks or footprints outside. No one knew about this storm. It's like magic. Nah, maybe you did this, didn't you, but how?" she asked.

James responded, "I didn't do this. I didn't tell anyone where we were going, I promise, my plan was for us only, and no surprises around every corner. I'm a good actor, but I'm not this good."

Jenny just had that confused look on her face as they finished decorating the tree. She kept looking at James with a smirk and a nod.

He looked at Jenny and announced very sternly. "I did not plan this." When they finished, they thanked each other for the time and agreed it was enjoyable, and they sat in front of the fire for a while. It was after a long period that they were doing something together and were able to put their sorrows away. After Toby, it was quite hard for both of them to think of anything but him.

James asked, "Do you believe me?" "Yes, I do. I know you would never strand us someplace on purpose," she answered.

There was a comfort in this place; something was quite familiar, giving them a comfy vibe. Jenny relaxed enough to start singing to one of the Christmas songs playing on the radio, it was soft, but James could still hear her.

"O Holy Night" is one of her favorites. She had a beautiful voice, and James was sure to let her know how he loved and missed hearing her sing. "I'm going to the kitchen to check out the refrigerator for food and get a glass of water. Would you like one?" he asked.

"Yes, please," Jenny answered.

After a couple of minutes, James called out and said, "There is a stew to be warmed up for a dinner meal with bread."

"Wonderful, someone has thought of us again. I told you someone knows we're here," Jenny replied.

James came in with the glasses of water, and he set them down on the table between the chairs. "Thank you," Jenny said.

There was still sadness in her voice. James overlooked that and found the book he had brought and started reading quietly to himself. Jenny began to hum some of the Christmas songs. Meanwhile, James grinned and continued reading.

He didn't say a word; he didn't need to. After about an hour or three chapters in his book, he noticed Jenny had gotten quiet; he could hear the wind blowing fiercely through the trees. James looked over and saw that Jenny had her head resting comfortably in the chair and fell asleep. He was pleased to see her sleeping. He was witnessing this comfort on Jenny's face after so long, and at that moment, he wished it to stay longer for the rest of her life.

Suddenly, one of the big gusts of wind hit the window and got James' attention. He looked at his watch, marked the page where he was reading, closed the book, and placed it on the table.

He worked very quietly in the kitchen. The smell of the stew and the homemade bread woke Jenny. She walked into the kitchen, "You did all this?" she asked.

"Yes, I did," James boasted. (of course, it was already made up ahead.)

"Please sit," James told Jenny, acting as a waiter, he even put a towel over his arm, and he pulled the chair out for her. She laughed and sat in the chair as James pushed her up to the table. He put the food on the table and sat. "Thank you," Jenny said. "You used to do this when we were dating."

"Me cooking for you," James gestured. "Yes, you did," Jenny affirmed. "Yes, it was one of my favorite things to do for you," James admitted.

Dinner was delicious and filling.

"It's getting dark outside; I guess I must have fallen asleep. For how long?" Jenny asked. James answered comically, "Oh, you mean your nap, something you never do. I think about an hour or about three chapters in the book I was reading."

Jenny laughed, "You're too funny."

James said, "I like it when you laugh; I need to do something to help keep you laughing again."

Jenny sighed, "I know, I just, l hurt so much inside still." "So do I," James said, "So do I. He continued, we're a work in progress, and I believe in us."

Jenny started to cry again and said, "I believe in us too. I'm so sorry." James stood up from the table, walked over to Jenny, and put his arms around her, "In time, we'll be ok," he said. They both hugged and closed their eyes for a while.

They heard a noise coming from the living room. James asked, "What now?"

They both went to the living room to find that the two chairs were gone, a loveseat sofa had taken its place, and the bins removed.

"This is so strange, and it has to be magic," Jenny said.

Then a noise from the kitchen came. They went back to the kitchen to find all the dishes cleaned up and two cups of hot cocoa with marshmallows and two pieces of apple pie, still warm from the oven.

"That was too fast. If this cottage is enchanted or haunted, I'm just not sure which, but it is here for us, I believe," Jenny said.

James replied, "I think you're right. It seems to be accommodating our needs, and they're doing a great job at making sure we don't figure out why or who it is."

They took their pie and cocoa to the living room and sat together for the first time in a while. James waited until they finished the pie to ask, "I'm going out on a limb here. Would you dance with me?"

Jenny agreed, she stood up, and James gently put his arms around her. They danced to three songs; Jenny then decided she was ready to turn in for the night.

As they headed back to the bedroom, James thanked Jenny for an enjoyable day of just being together. They had not spent such great day together, in months.

Jenny smiled and watched James get comfortable. She laid her head down and closed her eyes to sleep. She didn't speak a word. James said, "Maybe the weather will be better in the morning. But if it's not, I won't mind." He pulled up his covers and snuggled down to his pillow. Toby left a significant impact on the lives of the two, but this strange place made them understand that there was still a lot to explore in their upcoming life.

CHAPTER TEN

The following day, James woke up first. The sun was glinting through the window; it seemed beautiful weather outside. He got up quietly from the bed; he didn't want to wake Jenny.

She looked so good, still sleeping, he took a very long stare at her. She was so beautiful, and he still loved her so very much. He got a tear in his eye, so he walked out of the bedroom.

The smell of coffee and breakfast with those fantastic cinnamon rolls filled the air. James stopped to look out the window; he stepped back, shook his head, and looked out the window again. He went into the kitchen, got his coffee, and took a big sip. James wanted to make sure he saw what he thought he saw. James tried to know he was wide awake positively, so he took a second sip of his coffee. James looked out a different window; the view was the same. He thought, maybe I better wake Jenny for this.

"Jenny, Jenny wake up; you have to see this!" he shouted.

"See what," she asked, "what do you want?"

"Hurry, get up, and come here quickly," he hollered.

Jenny stood up, rubbing her eyes, "What is the emergency" Jenny asked?

"Look out the window," he shouted as he pointed and pulled back the curtain.

Jenny was still sleepy; she pushed her hair out of her face. She asked, "Coffee, I smell coffee. Where's mine?"

"Just look out the window, don't worry about coffee this minute," he demanded.

"Ok, it looks like there is another building," she said.

"Oh, we have neighbors; we couldn't see them in the storm," James said frantically.

"Wow! The storm has passed," Jenny continued. "May I have my coffee now, please," she asked.

James said, "There were no other buildings or houses here before, and our car is gone. Hello, aren't you a little curious?"

"Oh, I see breakfast," Jenny continued saying, "And the weather is clear, and we can't leave now. We have no car."

She started eating, "Nothing scares me anymore about this cottage," she blurted out, "We have been very safe here." There was a comfort in her voice, and nothing could dull her spark in the eyes.

Suddenly there was a knock at the door. Jenny stumbled a little, trying to make sure her robe was closed fully. James went to the door and yelled out, "Hello, who's there?"

There was no answer but another knock; James then opened the door.

A man said, "Hello, I'm Chip. How are you doing today," he asked.

"We're fine. What is it that we can do for you?"

James asked. "Oh, I'm sorry, please come in and give us a couple of minutes. Are we at your house? My apologies if we are," James said.

He stepped back and allowed Chip to enter. They headed to the bedroom to get dressed.

Jenny said, "It doesn't seem like he's upset we're here." James came out from the bedroom first.

He proceeded to ask, "Chip, who are you, and where are we? Are we in trouble for being here?"

Chip replied calmly, "No, you are not in trouble, and no, this is not my house. All your questions will be answered in a few moments. Would you both please come with me?"

Chip wasn't very tall. He had a rough voice, and he was strangely dressed. Jenny came out of the bedroom, made a sigh, and said, "Of course, we'll go with you."

She smiled at Chip. He had a kind face. Chip told them they wouldn't need coats; it was nice outside. James said, "Of course, it is," in a witty and sarcastic voice.

"It's been snowing heavily for two days; why wouldn't it be warm outside," he continued.

Jenny just gave him a look, and he stopped talking. Jenny stepped out the door first, "You're right, Chip, it is very nice outside here," she commented.

"Oh wow!" She gasped, "All these other buildings, houses, and shops, we couldn't see them yesterday at all. The weather was too bad. It's an entire town, look, James, it's beautiful here."

Chip just grinned and kept on walking.

Jenny asked, "How can there be so much snow and so much warmth outside? It's amazing."

Chip just shrugged his shoulders and said, "I don't know. It's always been this way."

They stopped in front of a massive cottage. It looked like something straight out of our imaginations and storybooks, with an enormous front door.

Jenny spread out her arms, "Look! I can only cover one door; who lives here," she asked Chip.

Chip just smiled and opened the door, "Please come in," he said, "And have a great day."

Jenny grabbed James' hand and pulled him in through the door. James was pretty hesitant, but Jenny's last tug pulled him through the door. The door closed behind them, and no one was there.

Jenny looked from side to side, then looked James right in the eyes and said, "I wonder what's next." They stood there for only a few seconds, which felt like hours, when they heard footsteps.

A white-haired white-bearded man came toward them. He introduced himself as Nick Claus. "So... your" Jenny started to ask, when Nick said, "Yes, I'm he." James shook his head, and as his jaw dropped, he said, "No, no."

"How? Your Santa, the real Santa… but there is no Santa. That's for children and toy sales," James said, pointing his finger and putting his right hand to his forehead and shaking it from side to side in total confusion.

"This is unbelievable." He mumbled and then asked, "Why us, and how did we get here? We were on our way to The Blue Spruce Spa."

Nick replied, "It's hot cocoa time; come with me." They followed Nick to the kitchen.

"Please sit," he said.

The table was a vast chunky pine wood with eight chairs. Jenny and James slowly sat, and Nick sat with them. Jenny held James's hand under the table; they both were frightened yet excited.

You could hear Christmas music playing in the background. No one spoke for a moment. It was almost awkward, total silence.

The smell of fresh cookies and hot cocoa filled the air. A beautiful woman in the kitchen turned around from a large stove and oven perfect for large meals, a dream kitchen, and said. "Hello, I'm."

Nick finished her sentence, "That's Mrs. Claus, my wife."

Mrs. Claus walked to them, "Just call me Jessica," she said with a pleasant smile.

At first, Jenny and James could not believe their eyes, and it seemed a beautiful dream to them. For the first time, after their son's death, they were actually slightly enjoying something, but were scared of it at the same time.

Meanwhile, Jessica put down a tray of fresh cookies from the oven. She went back to the stove, poured four cups, and brought them to the table, "Hot cocoa for everyone," she announced.

Before Jessica sat with them, Jenny looked over her shoulder and saw a large hutch made of heavy wood pine like the table. Neatly placed on the shelves were Christmas plates and mugs. She was impressed.

Jenny just knew someone had handmade this beautiful piece of furniture. It looked like someone had put their heart and soul into it.

Jessica sat down next to Nick and took his hand. She looked over at Jenny and James and smiled. She said, "I bet you're wondering why you're here."

They both nodded, and Jenny admitted, "Yes, we are curious."

Nick didn't smile this time when he looked at them and said, "Your hearts found your way to us, James and Jenny Lucks. We know your marriage is in trouble, but more than that, you as individuals are in trouble. We're here to help."

James was in shock; he stuttered out, "How, why, how do you know this?"

Jessica and Nick just laughed.

Nick asked, "Do you think we only keep a naughty and nice list? Divorce or separation isn't naughty list material. It might not be a separation on paper, but when you stop living for each other and just exist each day to get through, you lose. We want to help you. Do you want help?" Jessica added, "We do know your situation and that you both are worth saving. Marriage is about a partnership of 220%. Each partner gives 110% every day." Jessica proceeded to tell them, "First is caring for someone else before yourself. Next is respect for each other. Then comes support, trust for each other, and faith, something you have lost. Lastly, it is the love you have for each other. You have just lost your way home. This is why you both are still together after all this time. Most couples separate for good after losing a child. Your commitment and love for each other are so firm; that's why you both are here, and we are here to help. Don't you remember asking for help, Jenny?" Jessica asked.

"Yes," she answered.

"I stood by his closed-door four days ago and asked for help with my heart as I cried and hit the door." "James, you did something similar, didn't you," Jessica asked.

"Yes," James answered.

"I went to the cemetery, and I was praying and yelling as I walked around. I know he was so very small, and it wasn't his fault. I just couldn't stop yelling or crying."

Jessica told them that holding it in and not letting go is anger, not toward each other or Toby but at cancer.

James nodded and asked, "I am worried about my marriage. Can we get past this? We still can't talk about him. We can't even say his name, especially to each other. Yes, I did ask for help" James hung his head in shame.

"I've not been strong enough for both of us," he said.

Nick told James, "Forgive yourself. It's not for you to feel like you have to be strong enough for two, focus on your healing. Love your wife as she heals, and she has to love you as she focuses on her healing. Being each other's rock is part of marriage, but it must be shared. Marriages don't only carry the happy-go rides; there are rough patches in which both the partners have to love each other to the fullest. Here is where you begin to heal together with our help, but it is your choice. Do you want to move on?"

James replied, "Of course we do."

Jenny then asked, "What can you do for us?"

Jessica told her, "It's more what you can do for yourself. You must make the first move. You decided to go away together; that's a big first step."

"James," Jessica asked, "What do you want out of this?"

James replied, "I want my wife back. I just want to spend time enjoying life again with her, and in time maybe try for children again."

Jenny was shaking her head yes and said, "I have not thought of it earlier, but if I consider it right now, it will be the same I would want."

Jessica told Jenny that you must first forgive yourself for not sharing, and always remember you are in a partnership. There are no classes here; it's just living. If you're angry, yell at a tree or anything but get it out. Stop holding on to it. If you don't, anger will win. You will have to get out of the cottage every day. You will have to face some of the things you currently avoid. There will be challenges along the way, some more difficult than others. You cannot keep everything just to yourself. Things, in the beginning, will happen subtly, not fast; you will notice slight changes in your daily activity, you'll find your heart through others' kindness. The more you are willing to change, the easier it will happen. You must go out of your comfort zone. Once your heart opens, you will change rapidly. Lean on each other and talk to each other."

Jessica told them she had given them a lot of information and then asked, "Are there any questions you have that I could answer?" Jenny asked, "Why do you appear so much younger than we imagine you should be, and you're very wise? How's that done?"

Jessica explained, "We sleep 44 weeks every year and are awake eight weeks each year to get all our work done. We don't age when we sleep, so each year, we only age eight weeks. When we awaken, we have all the knowledge for the 44 weeks we have slept; this way, we're able to keep up with the times, as the old saying goes."

Jenny shook her head in disbelief. "This sounds like science fiction," she said.

Jessica agreed, "We don't even understand how it works; it just does."

James asked, "Where are we? I've never heard of this place before."

"We don't know ourselves; we just go on faith and belief in the magic of Christmas," Jessica replied.

"It's a fairytale, come to life," Jenny said.

James and Nick just listened to the girls talk while eating cookies. James then asked, "Will we remember this, or is our memory wiped clean, and will we go back to our normal life? Are we here to stay?"

Jessica answered, "Yes, you'll remember everything, and you will return to your normal life." Jenny asked, "What about our friends and family? Will they believe us?"

Jessica replied, "Your friends and family will notice that you're different when you get home, and it will be your choice whether or not to tell them. This may become a very private time for you, and you decide not to share it with anyone."

Jenny asked, "How long will we stay here?"

Jessica said, "You'll be in the village until Christmas Eve. And will wake up on Christmas day where you started. The next three days you can keep yourself busy, or you can choose to stay in your cottage. The choice is yours. If you don't do anything, you will not change. The village is a very delightful place and has a lot to offer. There are many activities scheduled, so there is a lot you can enjoy participating in. Getting out and participating will help you on your journey."

"The village is very charming from what I could see so far," Jenny said.

Jessica told her, "All the little shops are there for your enjoyment and transitioning. You will find twists and turns along the way. This way, you will work together. You'll find the unusual and the personnel in each shop. Memories will become a part of what you must allow yourself to experience. You must allow your imagination to see what you dream of and miss."

"You are welcome to sit by the fire with Nick for a while. It is a lot to process," she explained.

Jessica hugged Jenny and dismissed herself, "I always help with the dinner meal. It's promptly at 5:30 pm in the main hall in the center of town, where we all gather to have the best family and relaxation time. We don't talk about work; we have a 5:30 pm shut down. Games and movie time come after. Each night special events are planned after dinner." Jessica said, "See you later," and she left.

James and Jenny went with Nick to the living room and sat down. The main living room maintained the Christmas old-world charm. The fireplace stood about five feet at his highest point. It was made of river rock. A chunky pine mantle was above the hearth.

There were a couple of pictures and stockings hung. There were two oversized chairs in a deep red velvet with beautiful hand-carving arms and legs placed at each side of a loveseat sofa trimmed in the same carved wood and deep red velvet fabric; so very beautiful and Victorian. A fantastic homemade braided rug lay on the floor in front of the fireplace.

Jenny couldn't take her eyes off anything in the room. Nick told Jenny; to please look around, and she was ecstatic. The more she was getting close with the decoration, the more she was smiling. It was her joyous moment as nothing fascinated her in all these eighteen months of total distress.

Nick and James continued to talk. Jenny stood up and started inspecting every inch of the room. One corner had the Christmas tree, perfectly shaped and decorated so meticulously. She checked out the ornaments on the tree with much detail; she was stunned by the decoration.

The other side of the room had a large bay window with heavy red velvet curtains. They were pulled back so the sun would shine through. It lit up the entire room. She spent some time at the window looking out at the village; it was a beautiful view.

An exquisite large carved wood desk was placed in front of the window overlooking the living room. It was the perfect Santa's desk. You could tell it was very old. The legs were carved in a very detailed design. A beautiful one-of-a-kind snow globe sat on the desk in the center front; it was filled with trees and a reindeer-driven sleigh. Nick was using it for a paperweight. How clever, Jenny thought.

The end tables had beautiful stained glass lamps on them, with hand crochet doilies under them. Jenny went back to join them; she sat on the sofa next to James. There was a spark in her eyes as she was extremely excited about the things she was witnessing.

Nick began telling them that it was all their choice; they could still return to their car and finish their planned trip.

But Jenny was in a different world, and she abruptly said she would like to stay and work on themselves as a couple together. James nodded and said he wanted to work on them also. Nick told them they could talk with him or Jessica at any time they needed.

Nick asked them if they had any questions at this time. Both Jenny and James agreed that they were good at this time.

Jenny asked if she could take another look at some of the ornaments on the tree. With a big ho ho ho laugh, Nick said, "Take all the time that you need."

James asked about how the temperature stays so nice yet has all the snow. He also asked, "About that snowstorm that stranded us, was that planned too? Was this the plan for us? We have reservations at a resort." Nick just laughed and said, "My boy, slow down; your reservations have been taken care of. You'll be there next week as planned. Yes, the time stranded in a cabin snow blizzard were for your benefit. You both had no one else to talk or turn to. We need you both to be prepared to receive us so that we may help you."

Nick spent about an hour explaining a lot about the plan and how it all came together. He told them one big reason they were there was that they had lost belief.

"The miracle of Christmas is there for all who believe from their heart, not from a wallet. Your future is promising. We just need to show you that," Nick added.

He also explained how they surprised them with food at the cottage and how much he enjoyed keeping them on their toes. James chuckled and asked if the breakfast could continue; he loved the cinnamon rolls each morning.

Jenny turned from the tree, asking, "Where have you gotten all these ornaments."

Nick explained that "Everything on the tree was made in the village, some are very old. The treetop ornament came from Jessica's family; it was a wedding gift."

It was an exquisite hand-blown star with gold and silver accents. It twinkled from the lights and formed a rainbow on the wall.

"Jessica's father was a glassblower, in the town where she was born, in Italy. When we met, I was in my thirties, and she was only a couple of years younger. After we got married, we met a man who needed our help. We were placed here on the job. This man was called father "Noel." That's when our lives changed forever. We've never looked back or regretted it for one day. I can't imagine a better person to do this with than Jessica."

As he smiled, he looked over at Jenny; she said it was time for them to go and explore the village; he took a glance at his watch. Nick said, "Oh yes, we've lost track of time; you better go so you can start. I will see you at the evening meal."

Nick walked them to the door, "It has been my pleasure getting to know the both of you. Learn everything you can." Thank-yous and hugs came from both of them as they got to the door.

CHAPTER ELEVEN

When the door closed behind them, Jenny asked, "Can you believe where we are?"

She paused for a deep breath. She continued, "This place is only in our imaginations. This place is truly a Santa's village. Is it for real? James pinch me." So he did.

"Ouch!" she yelled out, and when she turned to look at James, he was laughing.

"Yes, I know, we're here. It's hard to believe," he answered.

Jenny grabbed James' arm and said, "I believe, and I'm a little scared, and I don't want to lose you. I'm ready to fight for us." James was in tears because he hadn't seen Jenny this vocal about anything so far. It was an achievement. They both did not know what it was all about, but they progressed with each passing second. They were becoming the old James-Jenny who were greatly in love with each other.

At the same moment, James hugged Jenny and told her he was ready to fight for them. He let her step away and then pulled her close again. James leaned down and kissed the top of her head. He closed his eyes, fighting back the flood of his emotions. James suggested that they walk around and see what is here.

Jenny stood in the street and took a long look at everything. She was contented and didn't want to miss any part of this village. Several shops lined both sides of the roads. Most of the shops were log cabins. You could see some houses behind the shops. All the rooftops were snow-covered. Very tall pine trees were all around, some you could see off in the distant mountains. James looked way down the road to make sure he could see their cottage.

"There it is," he said, "Right at the end of the road," and he pointed so Jenny could see.

"Yes, I can see; there it is," she replied. They both seemed to be happy.

Jenny asked, "Have you noticed all the shops seem to have a specialty theme? They are all so very personalized."

The glass shop was the first window they came to. The window was trimmed with a frosted look and glass snowflakes hanging. James stopped and looked into the window, "This looks like a beautiful shop; it's very festive," he said.

Jenny looked in the window with him and said, "Maybe there is a beautiful treetop like or similar to the one on Nick and Jessica's tree. Maybe we could buy one as our healing begins. Let's go in."

As they walked into the shop, they were greeted by name, and the shopkeeper introduced himself. The shopkeeper was dressed in the traditional holiday fashion, almost an Italian style. He was a little shorter than the average person. Jenny and James thanked him and walked in.

"Please help yourself, look as long as you'd like," the shopkeeper said.

Jenny whispered in James' ear, "Elf!!!" "No way," James said. They both chuckled and moved on. The shop was so cozy, and everything was made of glass—literally everything you could imagine.

Jenny asked the shopkeeper if they had any tree toppers "coziers" similar to the one they saw at Claus's home.

He nodded and disappeared. A short while later, an elderly man approached Jenny. He introduced himself as Jessica's Papa and said. "I understand you are interested in a glass star treetop."

"Yes," Jenny replied in pure surprise to meet him. He explained he only makes one of a kind and would ship it to their home when he is finished. They could use it next year. "Would that be ok?" he asked.

Jenny was so happy and grateful she hugged him and kissed his cheek.

She said, "Yes, Yes, and thank you so much. Oh, I forgot to ask, how do I pay you? I have a credit card in my cabin."

He said, "Your money is not good here. Anything you want is yours. Jessica and Nick make the rules. No payment is due. Everyone gets what they need or want. We have no crime, and it's a great life. It's very peaceful here."

James and Jenny were stunned to hear that for once, but they smiled greatly in return.

He then advised her to enjoy the rest of her visit and that all the shop items were handmade. Jenny walked away and started exploring excitedly.

Jessica walked in and asked, "Do you have a moment, Papa?"

"What can I help you with, my sweet daughter?" he asked.

Jessica and her father spent a few minutes together. She hugged and thanked him for his time, and she left. Jenny looked over and had noticed their affectionate love for each other, it warmed her heart, and she thought of her dad. It had been a great while since she had been close with any of her relatives.

Jessica's father walked over to Jenny to ask if she had any questions about the shop. She asked, "Is it ok if I ask a personal question?"

He nodded, and Jenny continued, "Did you leave your family to be with your daughter?"

"No," he said, "My wife passed away a few years before Jessica's marriage. They asked my son, his wife, and myself to join them. We decided that being a family together here was better than not sharing in this wonderful quest. I have my son's children here as well. We all own different shops."

"Thank you for your time," Jenny said.

Jessica's father was very kind. He answered all her questions and put her at ease, especially about family. While Jenny had been talking with Jessica's father, James had been off checking out the shop, and she was relating everything with her family and the connection that everyone had lost due to the death of their beloved Toby.

Jenny stopped and took a long look at the tremendously large tree in the middle of the store. It was roofed in white twinkle lights and clear glass ornaments. There were several other ornamented trees, each one different from the other. Some had colored glass ornaments, and others had large ornaments.

Jenny just kept saying wow at each turn she made. There was so much to see; Jenny wasn't sure where to start. She shouted out to James, "Are you enjoying yourself?" She heard a "yep" coming from the back of the shop each time she stepped forward.

She walked over to a large shelving unit on a far wall nook loaded with bells. Everything seemed amazing. Jenny picked up a small bell only to see, but there was no price tag. She walked over to the shopkeeper to ask about payment. "Remember here. There are no prices; if you want it, then it is yours," he replied.

"Oh, yes, I forgot," Jenny said, "Thank you."

She walked back to the bells. She saw an angel handle on top of a blown glass bell. She picked it up, only to discover that the bottom was a lace pattern. The ringer hanging by a gold chain was a heart shape; it was an alexandrite birthstone, and on the back was a name in gold, "Toby."

She stood in shock. Toby was the name of their baby boy who died shortly after birth, and alexandrite was his birthstone.

Jenny could not understand anything; she started shaking and crying out. James and the shopkeeper came running. James grabbed Jenny and wrapped his arms around her, and the shopkeeper grabbed the bell.

She stuttered as she told him to look at the bell. James took the bell from the shopkeeper and read the back; then, he returned the bell to him. "Wow! Just remember they know everything. This was meant for us. Jessica told us twists and turns," James said.

Then he added, "Our son is an angel in heaven. This is a reminder for us never to forget that."

Jenny was sobbing in great sorrow. James wouldn't let her go.

"We will face this together, my love, from now on; you are not alone. We have gone through enough, and now it's time to get up and face everything while holding each other's hands tightly, he affirmed her. Jenny took a deep breath and asked the shopkeeper if they could have the bell.

The shopkeeper wrapped it very carefully and said, "It will be delivered to your cottage."

"Thank you," Jenny said.

The shopkeeper handed Jenny a hankie; she nodded in gratitude and put on a half-smile.

Jenny explained to James what the shopkeeper had said about not paying for things they wanted. They spent another hour in the shop, holding hands and sharing what they saw with each other. They found a beautiful snow globe, and James was sure to have it put aside for them. They even saw a snowflake ornament that looked like their wedding cake topper.

The shopkeeper wrapped it up. James saw a beautiful carousel horse; he snuck it over to the shopkeeper and asked for him to wrap it up as a surprise for Jenny.

"It will be at your cottage," the shopkeeper replied. James put the back of his hand to the side of his lips so they would keep it hush-hush.

"Thank you," he whispered.

The shopkeeper told James that the shop next door had the very best nutcrackers. James appeared excited,

"Is it a…."

And before he could finish, the shopkeeper said, "Yes, it's also the best woodshop you'll ever find."

He hurried over to Jenny and told her about the shop next door. A train in stained glass caught Jenny's eye; she pointed it out to the shopkeeper; he nodded and gave her a thumbs up.

"Come on, Jenny," James shouted, "Let's go there."

He grabbed her hand and pulled her like a child out the door.

"Thanks!" Jenny yelled to the shopkeeper and waved as she went out the door.

Jenny shouted, "Wait. Stop, stop!" She pulled her hand away from his and began to tear up.

"Everyone here knows us better than we know us. It's the first time we have mentioned Toby's name, let alone see his name on something so personal, in all these months. That bell touched my soul, and it scares me."

James tried to console her, but she pushed him away. James led her to a bench close by, and they both sat down. Wrapping his hands around her hand, he held them as he spoke gently, "This has been the biggest blow between us ever, and we never talk about Toby. We act like he never existed, or even worse, we act like he's a forbidden topic. I never wanted to upset you by bringing him up. I was always trying to protect you. Jessica is right. I can't protect you alone. I need your help. I felt you never wanted to talk about him."

Jenny said. "I felt the same way about you. I needed someone to talk to, and I felt I couldn't talk to you. I was afraid to hurt you more. I thought you blamed me in a way for what happened."

"No, no, never, he was sick with brain cancer, we couldn't do anything except hold him and love him, and we did that," James said.

He felt bad that deep down, Jenny thought it was her fault. As for James, he never even thought about it for a split second.

He continued, "It's time to talk about Toby and look at the pictures as we do."

"Yes, I agree," said Jenny; she finally stopped crying.

"Let's go look at the other shop. We'll take our time and go slow," he said. They stood up, still holding hands, and began to walk toward the woodshop. They tried to keep the conversation going. They knew it was necessary. It was time to finally start talking. They both had been silent with each other for quite some time now. They talked to each other about a lot of things but never truly spoke to each other.

They stopped to look at the window of the woodshop.

"Awh look!" Jenny said. "It's a rocking horse just like the one we bought for Toby before he was born. It is behind the closed door in his bedroom."

"I had forgotten all about it," said James as he stepped closer towards the case, and watched it closely.

He then asked, "Are you ok with seeing this?" James motioned for her to come inside; Jenny nodded her head and went in the door. It was like they stepped back in time to another country.

The shopkeeper greeted them by name and then introduced himself as Jessica's brother Alberto. He was the shop owner. They all shook hands, and he told the couple to spend all the time we needed and enjoy ourselves. Jenny motioned for James to go on and look without her, saying that she'd be fine on her own.

Jenny turned to the front window display and fully inspected every inch of the rocking horse. She even ran her fingers through the mane. She patted the saddle and imagined her little boy sitting up there as she rocked him. He had red curly hair with a cowboy hat on his head. He was wearing fake little chaps and plastic pistols in his gun belt.

His cowboy boots were too big, but he wore them anyway because they looked like his daddy's. She grinned as he shot down the bad guys. He pointed to his sheriff's badge and told his mom,

"I'm Sheriff Toby, and I got 'em all; I got the bad guys, mom."

Her eyes were full of tears; she was almost about to cry. But, she managed a smile when she thought about the proud moment. She thought that they had gone in Toby's bedroom for sure and brought that rocking horse here. It looked the same as the one they got him, the colors and the old rustic look, even the weathered leather reins. She was in awe. There were no more tears, just a feeling of peace came over her when she thought of Toby, and a half-smile appeared on her face.

She mumbled to herself as she patted the horse, "You got all the bad guys, sheriff Toby, all the bad guys."

She lost track of time while she was busy being Toby's mom. The sound of the door opening caught her attention. It must be other shoppers. She thought as she glanced at them. She snapped out of her thoughts and came back to reality.

Jenny turned her head, and to her left, there was an entire wall of nutcrackers. She decided to focus her attention on the hundreds of little wooden soldiers frozen in time. The funniest one was Santa. It was hard to imagine Nick cracking nuts with his teeth. She chuckled as she pushed the handle up and down. "Hello Nick, nice to meet you," she said.

The one nutcracker that took her attention was the one that looked like a little boy dressed like a soldier; he had a sword and a hat too big and had red hair. She took it to Alberto and asked if she could get this one. Alberto said he could pack it up, and it would be at the cottage. It had a name stamped on the bottom; "Gustaf" she asked if that was the person who made it. "Yes, Gustaf is from Germany; he makes the nutcrackers," Alberto confirmed.

"Wow, that's amazing," Jenny was amazed.

Alberto explained that the workshop is in the back, and there are several woodworkers there. Alberto invited Jenny into the workshop in the back as she seemed very intrigued by it. She was able to watch Gustaf carving a nutcracker.

Jenny was amazed at how skillful Gustaf was. She stood there and made sure to let the workers know how much she liked their work. A few minutes later, she returned to the shop and thanked Alberto for all his kindness and for giving her the opportunity to look around the workshop.

She returned to the nutcracker wall. Jenny had never seen a horse nutcracker before, but they had one. One of the largest nutcrackers was also a lamp, and she thought how unusual it was. She saw a baby crib mobile. It was made with little nutcracker soldiers. She smiled and dreamed about the future.

James had spent a bit of time alone checking out a little wooden train, just a perfect fit for a little boy's hand. He imagined little Toby playing with it in their home. For a moment, he was Toby's daddy, and they were playing.

In a low deep voice, you could barely hear James saying, "Come on, Toby let's play." There was a small wooden track for it to be pushed on. He was lying on the floor with his little boy. They were taking turns pushing the train. A conductor's hat was lying on the floor, and he put it on. James started to tear up. He took a deep breath and wiped that tear dry. He grinned and sighed heavily before he decided to push that train around the track again, "Come on Toby," he cheered, "Let daddy help you move that train."

James made sure to be quiet enough not to be heard, but Alberto noticed James and made sure to make a note about the little train; it would be a surprise for him.

Jenny found James playing on the floor. She stayed silent for a while and just watched him. She didn't disturb him as she wanted him to have his moment. It filled her heart with joy and sorrow at the same time. Joy because she knew James would've been a great father to Toby, and sorrowful because it was a reality that he wasn't with them anymore.

Jenny could imagine James and Toby on the floor together. She had a smile and no tears. Just imagining Toby playing with his daddy made her heart fill with peace.

"Hello, I heard you," she said from behind as she approached James.

James looked up and asked Jenny if she had seen anything she wanted?

"Yes, I got a nutcracker," she replied. "I'm stopping to check the two Christmas trees filled with ornaments here in the center of the shop," she said.

"Can I join you, if you don't mind?" James asked hesitantly. He knew that both of them were grieving and needed privacy, so he didn't want to invade any private moments.

"Yes, of course, come on," Jenny replied.

She found a rocking horse ornament just like the one in the window, "I think I'd like that," she said.

James took it from her and gave it to Alberto, "Thank you," James said.

She had looked at a nutcracker ornament she liked, but she put it back. Alberto took notice of it, again.

Jenny spotted a beautiful big chair all hand-carved; she and James took turns sitting in it. The chair was very comfortable. It looked like something out of a castle. They took pictures of each other sitting in it. James said in his theatrical voice, "Hello, little girl. My name is Santa. Come sit on my lap."

Jenny giggled and jumped up in his lap. They laughed together like school kids.

"That was so much fun. Thank you for playing along," James said.

Jenny reached out and took James' hand. They walked to the front of the store, slowly looking at every little detail and taking it all in. Alberto recommended that they visit the coffee shop next door. They agreed as it sounded like a good idea.

The two decided to bid farewell to Alberto. They thanked him for all his help and kindness. Alberto held the door and pointed to the coffee shop across the street. He was the kindest man around!

The coffee shop was in a large log cabin with a front porch in the middle. There were two entrance doors, one at each end of the porch. The door to the left said, "**Coffee shop**." The other door said *"Bakery"* in fancy lettering and a sign under the window in the middle that simply said "**<u>Candy shop</u>**." How clever three shops in one unique spot.

You could walk to the bakery from the coffee shop by way of the candy shop. The coffee shop was quaint. The walls were unfinished logs with lots of shelving. Burlap bags of coffee beans from around the world filled the shelves. The far wall had tea, any kind of tea you could imagine. There were jars of herbs for you to blend with tea to make your flavors. The unfinished ceiling beams even had dried herbs hanging. The front of the shop had a section of chocolate drink blends for hot and cold. James knew if Jenny got in the chocolate shop, they'd never leave.

James was about to order something from the coffee shop as the aroma of the shop made him crave a nice hot cup of coffee. He turned to Jenny to ask if she wanted something, but she was off to the candy shop, and he knew she wouldn't be back anytime soon.

James got the coffee he wanted and a hot chocolate for Jenny, and he sat down. The shops had Christmas decorations with a rustic, comfy, and cozy vibe.

The seating area was in the middle with windows so you could enjoy the view. You could see all three shops from there. In the background, they were playing Christmas songs that made him nostalgic, and he instantly thought back to his youth days.

The tables were small, with two chairs at each table. Right under the windows were big chairs and a lamp for reading. There was also a small table for drinks. James could see Jenny from where he was sitting. He was enjoying watching her and about fifteen minutes later, Jenny returned, carrying a bag.

"I got fudge," she said, "Here try some. It's awesome, and it's made right there in that little shop. There was so much to choose from I just tried a few, but I got the fudge. It is the flavor of the day. They said tomorrow's special is chocolate-covered cherries and chocolate-dipped strawberries."

Jenny sat down and kept on talking about the chocolate shop. James could once again see her sparkling eyes. It was after a long time that she got excited about something so small. James smiled and just listened to what she said. This had not happened in a long time; he was enjoying every moment of this.

When Jenny's tales of the chocolate shop finally came to an end, James told her that the coffee and tea bars have daily specials as well. One of the shopkeepers brought Jenny a cup of hot tea.

"Oh, my favorite kind, thank you so much. I mentioned it to the gal at the candy counter." Jenny hurried and drank her hot cocoa and thanked James for getting it for her.

She looked James in the eyes and told him about her moment in the woodshop with the rocking horse and how she thought she was starting to find peace, but the pain was still there. Jenny also told him that she watched him playing with the trains.

James took a moment to stop Jenny and thank her for agreeing to come on the trip.

"We have a long way to go, and I know it still hurts to talk about Toby, but we've made such progress today. Thank you so much. I love you," James acknowledged Jenny's efforts.

Jenny agreed they had made significant steps today and that there was no way that the pain could go away. Toby had left a void in their lives, and they wanted to hold on to it as it was the only thing they were left with.

"We were like robots living our life day by day for the last year and a half. Today we've talked together more than we have in such a long time. We're even saying his name," Jenny said.

She started to get a little upset, and her voice broke a little. James stroked her arm.

He admitted for the first time, "I believe in this place all things are possible."

"I do, too," Jenny agreed.

"I need to go back to the cottage to have a big cry," she got up and left quickly.

James sat there for a while, he knew she needed time, and today had been overwhelming for them both. Grieving wasn't something one could do in a day. What had happened gave them sorrows for a lifetime, and it wasn't changing anytime soon. In fact, they wanted to grieve Toby for as much longer as they could. In no universe did they want to get over their own child; they just needed to make peace with the fact that it would hurt. They needed to grieve, and they needed to give time to themselves to let all the emotions flow properly.

He got Jenny's tea to go and walked back towards the cottage, and stopped at the flower shop along the way. James got some white roses and some poinsettias in a vase. When he came through the door, he heard nothing but silence. James looked in the living room, and Jenny had curled up on the love seat sofa with a pillow and was asleep. He found a Christmas quilt in the bedroom and covered her with it to keep her warm. James placed the flowers on the coffee table in front of her. He took his book and went to the kitchen, and sat at the table. Soft Christmas music started playing on the radio, so he let it play on.

After about half an hour, there was a knock at the door to let them know that the dinner was served and they should walk to the great hall in the center of town. James checked on Jenny, and she was waking.

"Who was that?" she asked.

He replied in a goofy voice, "I believe we were being invited to dinner."

"These flowers are beautiful, and I love them, thank you," Jenny said. She stood up from the couch and hugged James for the first time in a year and a half. James never wanted to let go of her now, but they had to leave for dinner.

They walked holding hands to the hall. Jessica greeted them and said,

"You will make so many friends here, relax and enjoy your dinner."

They got in line as it was a buffet, set especially for the visitors. James found some open seats for the two before they all got filled. The food looked good, and they both agreed they were hungry.

Jessica took a minute to check in with Nick. He asked if everything was going as planned?

"I believe we're on schedule. The twins are on their way now," Jessica snickered.

"Good," said Nick, as he nodded and chuckled.

"Little did they know how much time the four of them will spend together, now and in the future," Nick said.

"The twins are the best medicine we could ever find for them," Jessica said.

Nick patted her on the shoulder and said, "I love you, my darling wife." He then leaned over and kissed her forehead.

CHAPTER TWELVE

A petite girl came to the table where James and Jenny were sitting and asked if she and Timmy could sit. "Timothy's shy, but I'm not. He's my best friend. We're the same age, 5. Oh, I forgot to tell you my name… I'm Tomalina. You can call me Tommy," she said.

That little girl just talked non-stop. Tommy told them the candy shop, the bakery, and the toy shop were her favorite places in the village.

"Timmy likes the toy shop the best; he loves trains," she said. Tommy looked over at a lady motioning for them to come.

Tommy asked, "Can we see you tomorrow?" Both Jenny and James said "yes" in unison with no hesitation.

Tommy told them it was time for them to go to bed now, and they had to leave and join the other kids, and some were orphans like them.

"Orphans?" James asked, "How many of you are there?" he inquired.

"I think maybe ten."

She crawled up in James' lap, put her little arms around his neck, and gave him a big kiss on the cheek. "Thank you," James said.

Tommy got down, walked over to Jenny, and asked, "Can I kiss you too?"

Jenny leaned forward, saying, "I wouldn't have it any other way."

She got the best little hug and a kiss she had ever had. Timmy walked over to Jenny; she leaned forward and kissed him, he ran over to James. James leaned over and gave him a hug and a pat on his back and said, "See you tomorrow, little buddy."

A bell rang, and Tommy said, "We gotta go." They both ran off; Tommy was yelling to the lady waiting for them, "We made new friends, did you see them." She stopped and pointed to James and Jenny, who were waving goodbye.

"Yes, yes I do, now off to bed with you," she said as she waved goodbye to Jenny and James.

Jenny and James looked at each other in total confusion.

"Orphans," James questioned in a puzzled voice.

"I heard it; I'm almost afraid to ask how long they've been here. Tommy was so open she told us so much and didn't even know us," Jenny replied.

"I guess we should go back to the cottage; it is getting late," James said.

They walked back slowly to the cottage, holding hands all the way. James opened the door, and a powerful smell of hot tea filled the air.

"Wow," Jenny said. "They think of everything." They both grabbed a cup and went to the living room. The sofa was very comfortable, and they sat together. James said, "It has been a hectic day and so much for us to take it all in."

They spent a good hour talking about meeting the children and how they felt around the children. They both admitted it felt good.

"Let's put our dinner buddies aside for a bit. Reality set in for us today. Do you realize we haven't sat next to each other on any piece of furniture in such a long time?"

"We haven't sat together for a meal in almost a year either. Can you believethat?" James asked and then continued, "It's time to talk. Can you handle the memories and find the positive in them?"

"I have locked away all my feelings because of the pain it causes, but I have to learn to move with the pain. I remember Toby's smile and what looked like red hair, maybe. And I want to keep him in my memories forever. He was the brave one through it all. He rarely cried," Jenny said as her eyes started to get moist.

"You're right. He was the brave one. This memory hurts, but once we work through the pain in the memories, it should get easier to find the healing for us each day," James responded.

Jenny started to cry once again.

"I've never once considered the pain he was in, and he couldn't tell us."

James opened his arm, and Jenny slid into just the right spot, and he snuggled that arm around her. "I'm here for you always," he told her.

They both sat comfortably in front of a warm fire. James said, "This is how I want us to be, you in my arms," Jenny admitted it felt so good and that she had needed this for a long time too.

"I'm sorry I kept you away; please forgive me."

The radio suddenly came on, playing Christmas songs very softly. They both chuckled. It was very relaxing and quiet enough that they both fell asleep. James woke a couple of hours later, the radio was off, and he felt Jenny still in his arms. He woke Jenny, and they both went to bed.

CHAPTER THIRTEEN

The morning seemed to come quickly. James and Jenny woke up at the same time. Jenny was stretching and saying that she could maybe sleep a little more. She dropped back into the bed and snuggled her pillow.

"I believe that was the best night's sleep I've had in such a long time. When we went to bed last night, it was the first time in over a year that I didn't go to sleep thinking about tomorrow and reliving the pain," she remarked.

After their talk last night, James admitted that he felt a lot better, it helped him cope, and it was a great night of sleep for him. He grabbed Jenny's hands and pulled her up from the bed to him as if it were a tango and said in a western voice, "Come my darlin'. It's coffee time."

He let her go, and she fell back into bed. "I'm off," he said and headed to the kitchen, and Jenny soon followed.

Next to the kitchen, the other small table had a Christmas puzzle to be worked on.

Jenny giggled and asked, "Shall we?" James agreed, and they sat down and started the puzzle. They lost track of time because they were enjoying doing the puzzle together.

They took turns getting dressed and ready for the day, so they could check each other's progress, not wanting the other to do more than themselves. They were acting silly. Jenny was grabbing James' hands, trying to keep him from putting puzzle pieces into place. It was kind of like a child's play. It was getting close to noon; time had passed quickly.

"This has been the most enjoyable morning with you," James said.

There was a knock at the door, "Do you think it's the kids?" Jenny squealed as she clapped her hands lightly.

"Who is it," James asked. "It's me, Tommy," they heard in a tiny voice. James opened the door.

"I'm here too, ok," Timmy said.

Tommy had the biggest grin on her face as soon as the door flew open. James invited them in.

The two children ran inside the room and looked all around the cottage.

"Wow, what a pretty tree," Timmy said.

"Hey," Tommy said, "We need to go to the bakery and the candy shop."

"I'm hungry. Let's go, let's go," the kids yelled. The kids grabbed hands and pulled Jenny and James out the door, and they ran all the way. As the four of them ran down the street, hot cocoa, no candy, no cinnamon rolls, coffee, coffee coffee, were the words James was groaning.

As they got closer to the bakery, you could smell fresh bread. The bakery door was open, James stopped to take in a long smell. The kids pulled him and said, "Come on, we want to eat some of that smell."

James laughed, and they walked in the door. These kids were so adorable, James realized he hadn't enjoyed this much in a while.

Everywhere you looked, there was some kind of excellent baked goods some James had never seen before. The kids wanted chocolate chip cookies and hot cocoa.

Jenny sat with them at a table while James kept looking at everything. Someone from the coffee shop asked James what he wanted to drink.

He answered, "Four hot cocoas."

He also picked a variety of goodies from the bakery. Jenny looked at the plate after the kids and James attacked it like vultures. Jenny noticed how James was all in; he was thoroughly enjoying every moment.

"Well, I guess I should find something special for me and not just crumbs," Jenny commented sarcastically.

They all started laughing as she got up to go to the bakery.

James told the kids, "Jenny doesn't eat sweets too much, but she is a chocolate freak, and me. I like all sweets a lot."

The kids giggled at James; they seemed to enjoy it all a little too much. It seemed like one big happy family. Tommy asked Jenny to get her a brownie, and Timmy asked if he could have more cookies. James ran off to get more hot cocoas. Jenny was too excited to give the kids their treat. She couldn't wait to see their little giggling faces. She focused so much on the kids that she almost forgot to get something for herself.

The croissants caught her eye, and one had her name on it, so she quickly decided to grab one. Somehow, the little bakery items made Jenny excited. The four of them enjoyed eating till they were stuffed. They all sat back in their chairs for a few minutes to relax their tummies.

James, of course, being his newfound old self, was making gestures and full belly groaning, "Ohhhh, ouuuhh."

Timmy reached over and patted James's belly. "You'll be ok pretty soon," he chuckled.

Then Timmy proceeded to pat his belly and make the same noises. They all burst into laughter.

The kids said the toy shop was only two doors down and was the funniest place on earth.

"Then we should go," Jenny suggested.

The kids grabbed Jenny and took off, leaving James to throw away the trash. The shopkeeper said they would send a bag of goodies to the cottage for them later, James was asked about paying, and hands he put up his hands in the air, saying, "No money, gotta catch up with the group."

The shopkeeper said, "It looks like you better hurry."

James yelled, "Thank you!" as he ran out the door.

James saw Jenny and the two kids approaching the shop together and stopped to watch. He put his hands on his hips and shook his head. He imagined them to be one unit, a single happy family.

"This was family; we can have this," he said to himself.

James started yelling, "Wait up for me!" He sounded like a little kid and was acting goofy. For Jenny, it meant a lot as she loved this side of him, and it got lost somewhere between all the sorrows.

They stopped for James and watched him run in their direction. Jenny was shaking her head and laughing in disbelief. The kids were laughing in hysterics, and Timmy fell to the ground. He couldn't stop laughing.

James had to stop to catch his breath and motioned for them to go inside.

When he got to the toy shop window, he paused and watched Jenny with the children for a few minutes. He started to tear up. These were tears of joy. Jenny turned to see him outside of the toy shop window and motioned for him to join them. James nodded and wiped the tears, and hurried through the door.

"Show me the toys!" he yelled as he leaped into the shop.

"Oh my goodness," Jenny said.

The kids justlaughed.

Timmy grabbed James' hand and said, "This way, come on, look and see the train. It goes around on a track like a real train, and it looks like a real train too"

James loved trains; he told Timmy that it was his second most favorite thing in the whole world.

Timmy chuckled, then asked James, "You silly, what's your first most favorite thing?"

James replied, "Jenny is my first most favorite thing ever."

Timmy started laughing, "That's funny," he said. "You're my friend, aren't you?" Timmy asked as he took James' hand.

James said, "Yes, yes I am."

"Good, let's go to the back," Timmy said. The boys left to play with trains.

While Tommy and Jenny were looking at dolls, Jenny told Tommy about her doll collection that she had since she was a little girl. She showed her the kind of glass case she keeps her dolls in. She also showed her the kind of dolls she collected. There were a ton of dolls in the shop, and they all had a unique set of accessories attached to them.

Tommy got a funny look on her face and said, "You can't play with those kinds of dolls. They're in a case."

"Yes, I know; they're special dolls. That's why I keep them in a glass case," Jenny replied.

"One of my dolls belonged to my grandmother. She got it when she was a little girl. That makes her very old and very special. That's what they had to play with back then. That doll is made of china, it's a kind of ceramic, it's very fragile, and it has real people's hair on her head. Her dress is made of lace, like this doll," Jenny held up a beautiful baby doll dressed in pink lace. Her attraction towards dolls was too evident. It seemed that they had played a major role in her childhood.

Tommy asked, "What's this doll made of?"

"I believe she's a kind of doll you can play with."

Tommy hugged Jenny and then grabbed the doll and hugged it too.

Tommy told the doll, "We will be best friends." Jenny smiled as she watched Tommy with her new doll. She saw her little self in Tommy as she caressed her doll's cheeks.

Tommy asked Jenny about the books. They decided to go to the book nook to check it out. Tommy wanted a storybook and asked if Jenny could read to her. Jenny suggested they find a book together so they can pick the one both of them would enjoy reading.

Tommy found one of the books Jenny had written.

"Look, it says here that this book is written by some Jenny," she exclaimed.

"Yes, that's me," Jenny replied.

Tommy was amazed. She opened the book and started to read a little with her broken sentences. It was about friendship. Jenny was happy to see her book in the shop, and she was glad that Tommy had stumbled upon it. Jenny always wanted to make a difference in the world. She wrote this book so she could teach children about friendship, love, and kindness.

On the other hand, Tommy couldn't contain her excitement. She ran off to a comfy oversized bean bag on the floor, and Jenny joined her. They snuggled up together. Tommy got as close to Jenny as she could, and Jenny began to read. Tommy told her new doll to listen to what she was reading.

The boys were still playing with trains; the train tracks also mixed in a small car track. James hadn't even looked at his watch. He didn't need to, as they were having so much fun just acting like boys. Timmy went up to James and gave him a little push "You're in my way," he said.

James gave Timmy a little push back and said, "No, you're in my way."

They both laughed and hugged as they fell to the floor; Timmy got on top of James and claimed victory. They wrestled on the floor some. James tickled Timmy, and he squealed, "Help me."

They were both in a big hug laughing.

The shopkeeper interrupted them and said dinner would be served shortly, and he was closing for the day. James and Timmy could still spend a couple of more hours here together, but they were also very hungry as soon as they heard about dinner.

James thanked him for the best day of fun ever. They went to find the girls.

Timmy yelled, "I found them," and he jumped on the beanbag with the girls.

James followed and jumped on the beanbag to join them. James said, "It's dinner time, and we need to go; the shop is closing."

Jenny asked, "Why, can't we please just have a few more minutes with that pouty face."

They stayed there a few more minutes, and Jenny finished the book. All of them listened very carefully. As for Tommy, she told Jenny how much she loved her writing and admired her efforts.

"I want to be like you someday," she told Jenny.

"Well, I'm hungry now," Timmy shouted.

Jenny stood up with the kids; they all grabbed James' hands and pulled to help him up. James started moaning and groaning and acting like he couldn't get up. He then tugged, and the children fell on top of him. Jenny was laughing so hard her sides began to hurt.

Tommy asked the shopkeeper if she could take the doll with her; he nodded and smiled. The shopkeeper then handed a train engine to Timmy and said, "This is for you."

The children thanked the shopkeeper, and Timmy declared, "Dinner time, let's go!"

The children grabbed hands, and they were off. Jenny and James grabbed hands but decided to walk and watch the kids from behind. When they got to the hall, the line was way down; they didn't have to wait, they got their food, and Tommy said, "Come and sit with us. The other kids want to meet you too."

They got their food and sat with the children. The children asked many questions, and there were a lot of subjects discussed.

Jenny and James were in ecstasy; words couldn't describe how they felt. They didn't know they would enjoy the kids' company so much. Some of the kids sat in their laps, telling them their names and how old they were.

Jessica and Nick watched them from across the room. The toy shopkeeper took a minute to visit with Jessica and Nick and told them about the three-hour afternoon playtime in the shop. They were both pleased with the progress.

Nick said, "This is moving along better than we first planned." Jessica leaned over and kissed Nick on the cheek.

It was an ice cream social night, so everyone stayed in the dining hall. It was homemade ice cream, and the kids got to participate in the turning. When the turning got stiff, the kids made James pitch in. James, of course, hammed it up and acted like the strong man he was. He grunted and groaned. All the kids and some of the adults joined in on the fun. Once the ice cream was ready, everyone had to take their bowls up to the counter and make their own toppings.

All the kids put lots of candy on theirs; it was fun watching them load their bowls. Before the children left for bedtime, Jenny and James received hugs and kisses from every child and even a couple of high-fives.

Most of the adults thanked them for their help entertaining the children. Tommy still had the new doll she had gotten earlier in the day. She hadn't put it down; it was her new best buddy. Timmy was still carrying his train engine. You could see it peeking out of his pants pocket.

Jenny and James looked at each other, "Orphans," they said at the same time.

"Are we ready? Do you think we could do this?" They asked each other at the same time.

They saw Nick, but he was leaving so they decided to go and speak with The Clauses in the morning.

Jenny and James were wired up from all the excitement; they walked back to the cottage slowly. They enjoyed the night sky and each other's company. The aurora borealis surrounded the sky above them. It was tremendous and something neither had ever seen before. James took a couple of pictures so they could remember the sight.

Two cups of hot relaxation tea were ready for them when they walked in the door. They got their tea and sat in front of the fireplace. Christmas music was playing softly in the background. They were still on an exciting high with so much energy. They both talked for a while about the day and what each one of them had done on their own time with each child. They both agreed they hadn't felt a connection with any children since the loss of Toby.

"I must admit I feel a little guilty for having fun and letting go from thinking about Toby today," Jenny said.

She then asked with tears, "Is that wrong? Do you think Toby would have been like these children and all their little friends?"

"I believe so," James said, "And I think we would be enjoying doing these kinds of things with him."

James paused for a few seconds, then continued,

"I want to show you something. It's my picture of Toby. I keep it in my wallet, but I never take it out or look at it. I think it's time. It's the hospital newborn picture."

He took out his wallet and opened it to show Jenny the picture. She took the wallet from James' hands,

"Thank you," Jenny said in a weak and shaky voice, "I love that you showed this to me tonight, and thank you for getting us stuck in the storm."

"I'm going to have a hard time going to sleep; I still have so much energy," James said.

Jenny agreed, but it was getting late, and they wanted to get up early enough to talk with Jessica and Nick. They laid down. Jenny thanked the Lord for what was happening in their lives, the improvement, and the change. Then she heard a slight snore; well, James was asleep. She chuckled and rolled over.

CHAPTER FOURTEEN

James woke first, went to get his coffee, and sat and worked on the puzzle for about a half-hour when Jenny came out and got her coffee.

"Awh," Jenny put her arm around James' shoulder and said, "You're working on the puzzle without me; it looks so good."

"Do you still want to go and ask about the kids," James asked.

"Oh yes," Jenny replied without giving another thought.

"What about you," she asked.

"Yes," James answered, "I thought about it all morning; let's get ready to go," he said.

They made a quick stop at the bakery for a breakfast treat. James told the shopkeeper they were going to the Claus's that morning and wanted to know if it was appropriate to bring something or Jessica would have made it already.

The shopkeeper handed James a box and said, "Jessica asked to have you bring this when you came this morning."

James commented, "I guess she does know everything."

The shopkeeper grinned and said, "She's expecting you anytime."

"Thank you," James replied.

The couple hurried to Claus's cottage; they talked about the questions they would ask. They had mixed feelings of excitement and nervousness. "Adopting these kids," James said.

"Right," Jenny said, and then they fist-bumped.

They both said together, "Let's do this."

James raised his hand to knock on the door when it opened, and Jessica greeted them.

"Good morning, glad you came, come in, please. Coffee is on, and I'll take that box from the bakery, thank you," she said.

They followed her to the kitchen and sat down. Nick joined them in the kitchen. "What can we help you with today," he asked.

James said, "We want to ask about the orphan children. We would like to adopt."

Nick got a somber look on his face and said, "These aren't just any orphaned children; they are unborn children."

James grabbed Jenny's hand and said, "I don't understand. What are you saying?"

Jenny teared up and said, "I do, I understand; we can't adopt them. They belong to someone else."

Jessica walked over to Jenny and took her other hand to comfort her.

Nick said, "Let me tell you what all this is and what it means."

He took a deep breath and started to explain, "These children are going to families that are planning on having children. Timothy and Tomalina are twins, and yes, they are going to a family well deserving of them. These parents are not aware they're pregnant yet but will by next week, their Christmas gift this year." Jenny started crying, "I was so hoping for us," she stopped talking and continued crying.

Nick stood and walked over to comfort her. Jessica stayed by her side as she slowly caressed Jenny's back.

Jenny put herself back together and stopped crying. She looked up at Nick and asked, "Do you know where all the children are going? Will we ever have a chance? We are so hopeful now."

Nick smiled at her and said, "Where there is love and prayers, there is always hope and chance."

Jessica told them she had seen much change in them in only a couple of days.

"You're doing so well, and your time will come. When you leave here, you'll still have challenges to conquer."

Jenny stood up, hugged Nick and Jessica, and thanked them for everything they had done.

She then said, "The rest is really up to us."

Jessica nodded and said, "Yes, it is, my dear one, learn all you can with the time you have left. It will help you grow together every day." Jessica led them to the door as they were leaving and said, "Finish what you've started here. We just have given you the first push."

Jessica told them there were two shops they needed to see: a fabric and yarn shop that makes beautiful quilts and afghans and a metal shop. Lessons to learn in each shop.

Jessica leaned over and whispered in Jenny's ear, "Anything is possible if you only believe."

After they left, Jessica turned to Nick and said, "It was all I could do to hold back from telling them the twins are theirs as long as they continue the journey, and I believe they'll do it."

Nick said, "I believe they will as well." He continued, "You know the children did choose their parents this time."

Jessica admitted that James and Jenny were her favorites of all the couples they had helped, and Nick agreed they were special.

James and Jenny decided to go to the coffee shop. Jenny ordered the s'mores hot cocoa, and James ordered the triple chocolate cocoa. Jenny grabbed a couple of pieces of fudge. They talked about and asked the big questions. Was it too late for them to try and have a family?

James asked, "Are you ready to move on?"

Jenny replied, "I can overcome anything with you, I didn't remember that before, but I'm sure of it now." "I needed to hear that." He grabbed her hands and squeezed and continued speaking, "We have been concentrating on ourselves so much in the last few days I feel we are worth fighting for."

"I love you forever," they both said at the same time.

"We'll worry about children later; let's be a couple first. It's like we're starting over," Jamessaid.

He knew that healing was important, and it could only be done as a couple. They both needed to take their time and find each other again. Only then could they be a happy family. They needed to be complete in each other to start a new family.

"Let's go to the fabric and yarn shop and look around," Jenny suggested. She badly wanted to be busy all day and fill up her schedule with just anything.

The sign on the door said, "All things made by loving hands."

This intrigued Jenny. She entered the shop immediately and saw a yellow baby quilt with a rocking horse embroidered on it. It was lying just inside the front door. The shopkeeper told her she could customize it with a name. Jenny gasped; she held it up to her face, "Oh," she asked, "Would you please put the name Toby, no Sheriff Toby on it?"

Then she held it out for the shopkeeper to take. The shopkeeper nodded and took the quilt.

James was surprised. "Progress," he said.

Jenny said, "I plan to put it on the rocking horse and move it to the family room out where we are. I plan to open up the bedroom and repaint it to a neutral color."

Jenny looked at James and said, "I'm ok. For the first time, I can say my heart is ready. I know it seems like an overnight decision, but it's right; I feel it, and Jessica said it would start slow and change fast. I'm at peace."

She started to walk away. James found a wedding ring quilt; it had beautiful colors and would look nice in their bedroom back at home. The shopkeeper took it from James, and he asked her to hide it for a surprise. James asked for their last name to be put on it and the date. The shopkeeper nodded.

James then found an apron and busted out laughing as he read it. Jenny came running to see what was so funny.

"The lady of the house is always right; give her chocolate to change her mind."

He told Jenny, "You need to have this." Jenny laughed and agreed it was her, so they got it. She walked over to an area that had quilts made for babies. Jenny saw two baby quilts, one pink and one blue for twins. Jenny called James over and said she wished she knew where Tommy and Timmy were going. She would love to give the parents these quilts. James agreed it would have been nice to do.

"Let's move on. We can't dwell or be sad. We need to be happy after all; they'll have a loving family," James said.

The shop also carried hand-knit and crochet outfits for babies. Jenny pointed out how nice these would be with the matching quilts.

Jenny found a cowboy teddy bear. It had chaps, a hat, and boots. It brought it back to her memory of the woodshop. She felt happy and had no thoughts of sadness. She asked the shop owner if she could put Toby's name on the pant leg. The shopkeeper asked, "Should I put sheriff Toby on him."

Jenny grinned and said, "Oh, how thoughtful are you? Yes, and thank you."

The shopkeeper recommended the deli for lunch. It was next door, and they would enjoy the food. James thanked the shopkeeper and asked, "Can you read minds?"

"I am hungry," James told Jenny.

He was getting hungry, and the deli shop was next door. The shopkeeper had kept notes on all the things the couple had looked at. As they left the shop and said thank you, he contacted Jessica and told her all that had happened.

They sat on a bench before entering the deli. Jenny wanted to make sure James was good with how she was doing. He told her he believed they both had done so well and just knew they would have a great life together.

He said in his goofy voice, "I believe, my dear, our future is lookin' grand." Jenny laughed.

James got on his knees and was begging for food.

"You poor dear," Jenny said as she put her hands around his face. She loved that James was acting goofy even when the kids weren't around.

They decided to go into the deli before James melted away from starvation. They entered the shop and saw three deli cases filled with meats and cheeses from around theworld.

Places they have never seen or even heard of. They were allowed to sample so much; it was a platter with as much as they could eat. There were even hot rolls from the bakery ovens to make sandwiches. It was an excellent lunch. They decided to take it slow and savor the flavors. While they were eating, they overheard someone talking about a sledding party for everyone.

It was the big hill at the edge of town. The best hill we have, they heard. So they decided they better ask about it. They were invited. They asked the shopkeeper about their leftovers.

"I'll send them to your cottage," he said.

"Thank you!" they yelled as they ran out the door, like a couple of kids.

They followed the crowd to the big hill. Wow, it was a beautiful spot with evergreen trees all around. People were grabbing toboggans from a huge rack. James grabbed a toboggan as well and yelled to Jenny, "It's our turn to go, come on."

Jenny sat down in the front, and James did the 1-2-3 push and jumped on the back. He and Jenny screamed like children down the hill, and at the bottom, the toboggan fell over, and Jenny went face first in the snow. James put out his hand to help her up while he was laughing hysterically.

She pointed at him and said, "You did that on purpose."

"Haha!" James laughed even more.

She grabbed his hand and stood up. She jumped up and kissed him, "I love you."

She started running up the hill and said, "the last one up buys dinner. He ran up the hill after her. Pulling the toboggan behind him, and she was at the top, jumping as the winner. James got to the top of the hill, pushed Jenny to the ground, and said, "I'm a bad loser."

Jenny was lying on the ground laughing and still saying she was the winner. James dropped down on the ground laughing. He rolled over on top of Jenny, looked her in the eye, and said, "I love you," and he kissed her.

After a long look in each other's eyes, Jenny smiled, "You're just a sore loser," she said.

They rolled around in the snow a little bit.

"I'm ready for another wipeout; let's go," Jenny said as she ran back to the starting point.

They made another trip down the hill. It all felt like they were back in time, to the days when they were dating.

"I'm having so much fun," Jenny said. She giggled just like a little kid. They made two more trips down the hill and decided this was the last trip down.

James was putting away the toboggan, and they both heard someone come running up the hill yelling to everyone, hurry! Snowball fight!

"It's the annual snowball fight; it's starting now in the center of town!"

Jenny yelled, "A snowball fight!" and she ran off, leaving James behind. James watched her runoff. He shook his head, laughed, and ran after her. He saw his old Jenny returning to him. Once she started having fun, there was no stopping her.

James joined the crowd running to the center of town. When he got there, he was out of breath; he bent over, put his hands on his knees, and was trying to catch his breath. He was also trying to find Jenny in the crowd. Snowballs were flying everywhere. Jenny found him first and ran up to him. She said she hadn't seen the children here. James agreed. He no sooner got the words out when he got hit in the chest.

Jenny started to laugh. "Who did that?" She turned her head and saw the children holding on to each other, laughing.

James saw them too, "Ok, this is war!" he shouted using his crazy voice and gestures.

The snowball fight had begun. Jenny got a little too far away from James, and he hit Jenny right upside her head. She had snow on her face and her neck. Jenny looked at James, and he was laughing and pointing at her.

"Game on," she told him; she pointed her finger at him. He did the eyes on you. Hand gesture and tried to hide next to a light post.

She ran over to the kids dodging snowballs, "I'm here to join your team," she said.

"Look at him. She told the children he was trying to hide. You can't hide," she yelled to him.

Jenny devised a plan of action. She crouched down and told the kids, "Let's all get a snowball each and throw them all at the same time. One of us will hit James."

So they gathered up snowballs. "Ready aim," and they all jumped up, and Jenny yelled, "Fire!"

They threw their snowballs at the same time. James must have gotten hit with almost every snowball thrown because when Jenny was counting down, a few villagers joined her team as well. Now she had the whole army gathered to get James down.

He played along with them and gave the kids a show; he threw his hands in the air and fell over into a snowbank. The kids ran and jumped on him. So many people saw them and started throwing more snowballs at the pile. Jenny ran to them, and through all the noise, Jenny asked if James was ok.

"Yes," he said, "Never felt better. I haven't had this much fun since college."

Jenny agreed. She didn't remember laughing this much in a long time. Now it was them and the kids against all the villagers, and the fight resumed.

Soon the bell rang for dinner. They were all covered in snow, and Jenny started helping clean the children up. Everyone slowed down and started heading to the great hall for dinner. Jenny held back, hiding a couple of snowballs with James' name on them. When she had scoped out just the right moment and waited to make sure she wouldn't hit anyone else, and when the timing was perfect, she would unload three snowballs on James. It was the ideal time he turned to talk to her, and Jenny let them all loose on him; every one of the snowballs hit him.

"I got aim," she laughed and ran up to him to help clear some of the snow. They hugged, kissed, and laughed together.

The dinner menu was hot biscuits from the oven and beef stew, the perfect meal for a winter's day. You could smell hot apple crisp for dessert. Jenny and James sat with the kids again. They all were still pumped up about the snowball fight and couldn't stop talking about it.

The kids were talking about how crazy James is and how much fun they had with them both. It seemed like the best party was at their table. Before they knew it, a lot of people joined them at the table. Kids were on the laps of the adults, and everyone was telling stories.

"Clean up the tables; it was game night," came over the loudspeaker.

They all cleared up the mess within a few minutes. Board games came out of the closet and onto their tables. Jenny and James were given a game that could be played with several children on the floor. Twister.

"Oh my goodness," Jenny shouted.

"I'll do the spinner, and you and the kids can twist it up."

James started to stretch, getting himself ready for the game, he was doing it in comedy style, and the kids ate it up. They all started copying him. When the games began, there was an announcement that they had ninety minutes to play. There were three mats put out, so they had enough dots on the floor for all to play. There were three adults and three kids per mat. The first team to drop would be the loser, the last team standing would be the winner.

Jenny spins, "Left foot blue."

James started teaching his team how to talk smack. They started talking smack to the other two teams. James was telling everyone else how good his team was and how bad the other teams were. Pretty soon, all the teams were trashing the other teams, all in good fun.

"Right-hand yellow." A scream came from team three, and a lady said, "Move your hand over there."

Everyone started to laugh. It wasn't long before, a crowd gathered around. They were choosing teams and cheering on their favorites. The first team fell, everyone started laughing and applauding, then James started teasing them. Well, guess what happened next "Right foot blue," and James and his team fell simultaneously. Team 2 was the winner. All the kids piled up on top of James.

After a while, the call came for the kids to go to bed. The children resisted and refused to go back to their beds. For them, it was too soon as they were having a lot of fun.

Hugs and kisses all around and two little "I love yous came" from Tommy and Timmy.

Jenny began cleaning up, and James came up from behind her and put his arms around her, and kissed the back of her neck.

"You will be the best mom ever," he whispered in her ear.

He continued, "I think I'll make a pretty good dad. What do you think?"

Jenny replied, "You'll be the greatest dad." They just looked into each other's eyes, and happiness shined on their faces.

"Hey, what do you think about heading back to the cottage, maybe get a hot soak in the tub," James asked Jenny.

"Oh, that sounds fantastic," she said.

Walking back to the cottage, they held hands and talked about how it had been such a busy day. They didn't even go to the metals shop. Jessica had told them how great it was; maybe tomorrow they would go.

"Oh, and dinner tonight was fantastic," James said. Jenny agreed.

They got to the cottage. James stopped at the steps and held Jenny's hand, "We can't ever go back to where we were. Today made me realize how our life could be like. I want to continue moving forward, and I want you by my side with or without children."

Jenny snuggled into his arms and said, "Forward is the only way for us to go, we might find a pebble in our road from time to time, but we'll kick it out of our path. I'm in it to the end. I want to grow old with you. You are my true love and my soulmate."

James wrapped his arms even tighter around her with all his strength, "I never want to let go." Jenny replied, "But we have to go to bed sometime tonight. Until then, hug me. Please."

"My pleasure," James said, and he opened the door.

While Jenny was in her nice warm bath, James made tea for two. After hot tea and time in front of the fire, they went to bed and slept in each other's arms all night.

CHAPTER FIFTEEN

In the morning, they opened their eyes at the same time. James had a couple of sore muscles from yesterday but said it was the best night's sleep ever.

She asked if they could just stay in bed for a while and snuggle. James agreed to a lengthy cuddling session. Neither of them wanted to get out of bed as they were tired from all the playing from yesterday.

After about an hour, they got up to find coffee ready for them. Jenny raised her eyes to the ceiling and said, "Thank you, Jessica."

James raised his cup and said, "You're a blessing Jessica."

Jenny replied, "Let's go to the bakery for some breakfast."

James ran to get dressed. Jenny followed. They stayed hand in hand on the walk to the bakery. After ordering their breakfast, they found a table and sat down. Jenny told James she was happy she got the quilt for Toby and wanted to open up his bedroom when they got home. She wanted to honor Toby, not close him out of their lives. We have a lovely photo we took of Toby right after he was born, and she wanted to frame it and display it with all family photos for the future. James thought that was a great idea, and he would help her do it. He asked if he could pick the paint color for the room.

"Yes, you may, but I'd like it to be a neutral color," Jenny said.

James told her he wanted a real Christmas every year from now on. The lights, the decorations, and the happiness.... he wanted to experience the real family charm on Christmas.

"Let's have a party as well and invite friends and family. I want to live again."

"Yes, let's do that," James replied. He didn't hesitate for a minute and was glad that Jenny liked his idea of celebrating the occasion together as a family.

"Did you realize today is Christmas Eve, and tomorrow we leave for the spa?" James asked.

Jenny said it had all passed so quickly she had lost track of what day it was.

"What do you think about us building a vacation cottage like ours near here on a lake, so we as a family can go to visit?" Jenny asked.

"Oh, wow, that sounds great. I can take our kids fishing and boating. Yes, yes, let's do that," James said excitedly.

They talked about what they should do today and decided to visit the metal shop as Jessica suggested. They finished their breakfast and decided to leave. "Thank you so much you've been so kind to us, and the food was fantastic," Jenny said.

She shook hands with the shopkeeper as he wished them a pleasant day. Before they got out the door, the shopkeeper told them that everyone went to the tree lighting that night after dinner. They were both very excited and said they wouldn't miss it for any reason. Whatever activities they've been a part of so far have proved to be great for the two. So, they were ready for whatever came next.

The metal shop was across the street. It had a very different window from the rest of the shops, but it fits the village theme. The window and door had a metal awning over them. It was unique; it was made of copper and was very shiny. It had a design punched in it, a Santa sleigh, and reindeer. Jenny and James took a long time to check this out.

Neither of them had ever seen anything like this before. The edging came down over the sides and had a beautiful lace pattern on it. The front door was copper with a blacksmith's picture punched out in it. The blacksmith was Santa. The sign in the window said, "All metals are worked here." It listed all the things that they made.

Jenny and James stepped inside the shop and noticed the metal shop had jewelry and platters, plaques, and signs.

Jenny found a sign, and the shopkeeper told them he could custom it by putting their last name on it. "The

Lucks Family-Great for our future cottage," James said. Jenny went to look at some serving platters. She then noticed an area with bells and was in awe of the workmanship on them. Jenny even saw a shelf of metal nutcrackers. It was astonishing all the items they had. She saw a train engine very similar to the one they had gotten for Timmy. She motioned to another worker in the shop and asked for the engine to be sent to their cabin.

"It's a surprise; please hide it," Jenny requested. She really wanted to enjoy the look of James' face when she would give him the gift.

James noticed a bracelet that had a boy's and a girl's silhouette heads on it. He asked the shopkeeper to engrave a name on each one and take it to the cottage later. He paused and asked if he could get a third silhouette, a boy with another name on it too. The shopkeeper was very happy to do that.

Jenny spotted a beautiful platter with a picture of Santa and a sleigh with reindeer.

The shopkeeper kept notice.

Jenny asked if they could go back to the cottage until dinner, work on the puzzle, and spend time together in front of the fire. They strolled back to the cottage holding hands.

"I just wanted some downtime with just you and me. I'm excited about the tree lighting tonight. I've never been to one before," Jenny said.

James made two cups of hot cocoa, and they sat down to work on the puzzle. James was putting in the last few pieces. He noticed Jenny was very quiet. James asked her if something was wrong. She said, "No, I'm just feeling a little romantic. Could we sit in front of the fire?"

"Of course," he found a little wine and some glasses. They enjoyed some time cuddling up on the sofa. Christmas music was playing softly in the background. Before too long, they found themselves on the floor cuddled up with each other. They had been back for about three hours when there was a knock at the door that startled them. They must have fallen asleep in each other's arms as they had no idea what time it was. They stumbled to get up and get it together so they could answer the door.

It was the children asking if they would come out and build a snowman. Jenny and James couldn't get out the door fast enough. The street had people lined up on both sides and piles of snow everywhere. All the children had been paired with adults for construction. There were several boxes filled with clothing for the snowman.

Tommy and Timmy insisted on making a lady snowman. Timmy ran to the chest and got a big floppy hat and a silk flower. Tommy told him they needed more than that, so she ran to the box and found an apron and a rolling pin.

"We need sticks for arms and coal for eyes," James said.

"We need a carrot for the nose too," Jenny added.

That stuff was in another box, and Timmy ran to get it. They both had just woken up, but they were happy to be out there for the kids. They both started to immerse themselves in the task and were rather enjoying it.

Timmy came back with his hands full of stuff; he even found a scarf on his way back, so he picked it up. He was so proud of himself. They all hugged him for a job well done. The bell rang for everyone to start building. The team next to them just so happened to be one of the twister teams. James started his smack talk again to that team.

Tommy tugged on his pant leg and told him to stop; it didn't work last night they won. Jenny laughed so hard she fell over in the snow, and James started throwing snow at her.

"This is a contest, Timmy," he said, "Get to work."

The four of them got back to the snowman "snowlady" business. Tommy said they needed to name the snowlady.

Jenny said, "What about Noel?"

The kids jumped up and down, clapping their hands; they thought it was a great name. James told them to keep working without him for a minute, and he left.

"What are you doing?" they yelled. They kept on working, and they needed to do the best job ever. James ran into the metal shop; he was out of breath as he rushed in a hurry. He asked the shopkeeper if he had a sign with Noel written on it. There was one, and the shopkeeper gave it to James. Out the door, he went. "Hey, look, we have to win with this sign; it has her name on it."

The kids were so excited; Timmy grabbed the sign, "The snowlady liked it too," he said, and he put it in place at the bottom where all could see.

They continued building, rolling, and packing snow around a giant ball. James lifted the middle ball, acting like it weighed a ton.

"Faker, faker!" the kids yelled.

Tommy said she needed one more on top. Timmy had already started rolling the third ball. James lifted it, and the kids started to pack around it to make a sturdy neck.

Timmy took the scarf and put it around her neck. Jenny put her eyes and nose in place. Tommy got the apron and asked James to help her. So together, they dressed her. Jenny got the stick arms and gave one to each of the children, James did his 1-2-3, and they put it in her arms. Jenny placed the hat on her head. Finally, Tommy needed help to put the flower on the hat. James picked her up and held her as close to the hat as he could. She placed the flower on the hat, turned and wrapped her little arms around his neck, and told him, "I love you."

"We are done!" the children started yelling, then other teams began finishing and screaming; they finished as well.

Snow People were lining each side of the street.

There was even a snow bride and groom. Everyone started walking around and looking at all the snow people. There were a lot of oohs and ahs. Jessica stepped out from her cottage and started looking around.

Someone said, "She's the judge."

The dinner bell rang, and everyone headed in for the big meal. Jessica remained behind and continued to observe all the snow people that were made. She was amazed at all of them being so different. She was delighted at how creative people could be.

James took a minute to tell the kids how proud he and Jenny were and that they had done a fantastic job. No matter what, they had worked as a team and had fun in the process, and that was the most important thing of all.

They went inside the dining hall to see the most beautiful meal ever—a complete turkey dinner feast with all the fixings and a dessert buffet.

The kids started to lose their minds. They wanted to eat everything they saw.

"Dinner fit for a king," James declared.

The children were asking for Nick, so James asked and was told he was never seen on Christmas eve, and he was already on route to fulfilling children's dreams around the world. Dinner had finished, and the children announced it was time to light the tree.

Jessica was already waiting at the switch. She told the crowd she couldn't decide on a winner; there were so many fantastic snow people. She was pleased with the participation and the variety of designs. This was the best year they ever had. She thanked everyone for the love and the commitment they've always shown. Jessica announced that the Noel Snow Lady was at the top. The crowd cheered for the team as James walked around bragging about his team. Jenny and the kids were just as pumped as their hard work paid off. Still, it was James' idea to add a nameplate to the snowlady which stood out, so he bragged all he wanted.

Everyone settled down and turned to the tree in the center of the town. James put Timmy upon his shoulders to see better, and Jenny did her best to help hold up Tommy. This was the grandest tree Jenny had ever seen.

She whispered in James' ear, "I don't think I have ever had a better vacation."

Jessica instructed everyone to come around this huge tree. Everyone shuffled around and got close together.

Jessica did the countdown and said, "Let the tree light up Nick's way home."

She flipped the switch, and it was beyond beautiful. It would light all the way home. There were cheers and applause. So many words were spoken about the tree, and suddenly someone began to sing, "Oh, Christmas Tree," and everyone joined in.

Hot cocoa, cookies, and brownies were set up on a table for all. The crowd sang three more songs together. It was quite the Christmas Eve. James and Jenny were not expecting such a grand end to their year, but there was one more surprise waiting for them in store.

The children finished their treats, and it was time for them to go to bed— there were hugs and kisses from all the children as their way of showing gratitude.

Timmy and Tommy spent the most time with hugs and kisses for Jenny and James. Timmy was up in James' arms with his final hugs.

He kissed James and whispered, "I love you, daddy." James was stunned. He froze as soon as he heard those words and didn't know what else to say. He gently put Timmy down and waved goodbye.

Jenny was bent over, getting her hugs and kisses from Tommy, and said, "I love you, baby girl."

Tommy whispered in Jenny's ear, "I love you, mommy."

Jenny stood up in shock and put her hand over her mouth. She was in disbelief. Tommy waved goodbye; Jenny waved back. She looked over at James, and he had a look on his face that showed Jenny how he felt. Jenny couldn't tell him what Tommy said. She didn't want to hurt his feelings.

James didn't want to upset Jenny either with what he heard, so he knew he couldn't tell her. He knew he couldn't face another setback after making progress; she had improved a lot, and he didn't want to break Jenny's heart.

The crowd was starting to clear. So many people came up to them, hugging and wishing them the very best in their future.

Jessica came over to them finally; she gave them both a hug and said, "This is your chance. Make the very best of your time together forever. You have shown love to others and have been loved by others. Find your intimacy with each other in that you will find your strength. Tomorrow morning when you wake up, the cottage will not be here. It will be back where you were when you got stuck in the storm. You will have until one in the afternoon to leave."

Jessica assured them all would be well and that they would remember all that happened here.

"You'll be anxious to return home, and right now, your heads are spinning. Use that energy for each other."

Jessica hugged them both again and told them it was like they were just part of the family here with them, and she couldn't express how happy she was to have them both here.

She took an extra minute to talk to Jenny; after another hug, she told Jenny, "Children will come in time, don't ever give up hope."

They returned to their cottage. This time, they walked very silently, and as soon as they reached their room, they both started crying and could hardly stop. They kept holding on to each other.

Jenny said, "I feel whole here; I don't want to leave."

James agreed. Two cups of hot tea were waiting for them. They cuddled up on the sofa together. Then they decided to finish their trip. The spa would be the perfect place for the two to rekindle. They both talked about how much they've grown and what they learned about each other's needs. He looked into Jenny's eyes and she into his.

They started kissing with passion. Jenny pulled away and started crying.

James asked, "Are you ok?"

"No, no," she replied. "'I'm sorry if you're not ready," James said.

Jenny, through tears, said, "No, I'm so sorry it's taken me this long. I'm so ready to start now."

She put her hands to his face and started kissing him. He stood up and picked her up, and carried her to the bedroom. Her tears ended and soon turned into passion.

After about an hour, James went to the kitchen to get the wine. He found their glasses from earlier in the day and refilled them. James checked the fire, and it was perfectly lit. He returned to the bedroom and jumped right into Jenny's arms.

CHAPTER SIXTEEN

When the sun shone through the window, they awoke still wrapped in each other's arms. They started kissing again; James said, "It's still early." We don't need to get up."

Jenny agreed; it was too early for her to leave James' arms. She wanted to stay in them a little longer. His presence made her feel safe and kept her warm.

About an hour later, they heard a noise in the kitchen and smiled at each other, "Someone's making coffee for us," James whispered.

Then the aroma of coffee and cinnamon rolls filled the air.

"I'm super hungry," Jenny said, so they grabbed their robes and hurried to the kitchen. Jenny looked out the window and said very sadly, "The village is gone. We're in a wooded area, and our car is parked out front. There was a little snow but nothing like what got us here."

"Jessica did tell us we would return to normal today," James said as he could hear the disappointment in Jenny's voice.

They walked to the living room, "Merry Christmas, my darling Jenny," James said, as he was acting it all out like he was in a play.

The arm gestures and all. Jenny laughed so hard at him, "You're crazy. That's one of the reasons why I love you."

James turned on the radio, and Christmas music was playing; James continued being silly. He started singing in a silly voice and grabbed Jenny to dance. He spun Jenny around, and she spotted something.

She squealed and started running in place with excitement and clapping her hands like a little child and said.

"I think we have gifts. Quick, look under the tree! Maybe they're for us."

James reached under the tree, "They are for us," he said.

They both sat down on the floor and started opening the gifts like kids. Jenny opened the bell. It's the one with Toby's name on it,

"Wow," she put her hand to her mouth and said. "I wasn't sure how I would react seeing it again. I was so upset that day. I forgot that I did ask to keep it. They knew all along I would see it again today, and we were supposed to have it."

James opened one with his name on it, a small wood train, it was the one he liked so much. Jenny opened the rocking horse ornament that she loved. James got a triple hot cocoa mix that he enjoyed. Jenny opened another one that had her name on it, and it was a wedding ring quilt. She was looking over every inch of it, "beautiful" is all she could say.

"Jenny," James said, "That's from me, for our bedroom."

Jenny noticed the name and the date. She leaned over and kissed James.

"How thoughtful of you," she said as she handed him a gift box that was from her.

He opened it up so fast, and "wow," was all he could say. It was a metal locomotive engine, a very old one.

Two boxes said do not open until February 14th; they were even wrapped in red paper.

"Ok, Jessica, we'll wait. You're hilarious," Jenny said as she looked at the ceiling.

One gift was still left, and it said: "From James to Jenny."

Without wasting another moment, she opened it, and it was the bracelet with three children's silhouettes on it, one boy with Timothy's name and a girl Tomalina and another boy with Toby's name on it. "Oh," Jenny cried out, "You couldn't have given me anything better. I love it."

She began to cry. She put it to her heart then handed it to James. She put out her wrist and asked him to hook it on for her.

James said, "This is for all the children we have known in our lives that have meant something special to us."

"Is it ok, Jenny?" he asked.

"It's better than ok," Jenny said. She reached over and cupped her hands to his face and kissed him.

They stood up kissing while James told her they had time before they needed to pack. They returned to the bedroom for awhile.

They spent time together, discussing the gifts and asking when they got stuff packed for each other. The radio soon announced that it was eleven O'clock. Jenny and James decided to start packing and get the car loaded. James carried the first load out, and Jenny made sure all their gifts were carefully packed in a box. There was also a box filled with the items they had asked to keep. Jenny did a second look around the bedroom to assure them they hadn't left anything behind.

She heard a noise in the kitchen. She came out of the bedroom asking, "James, what are you doing in the kitchen?"

Only he wasn't there; it was the baker from his shop with a box of treats and lunch sandwiches from the deli. He also had a package from the candy shop. He said to her, "I'm not supposed to be here or to be seen here. But I wanted to say thank you for showing us in the village about love and growth together. We've enjoyed you both and will remember you forever; you're an extraordinary couple."

Just then, James walked through the door. With a puzzled look on his face, he asked, "Is this your cottage, and we just got to stay here."

The baker said, "Yes, it is. I got married two weeks ago, and now it's open. I must go. I've stayed too long."

"James," the baker said, "There are extra six cinnamon rolls just for you. The candy shop sent fudge and chocolate-covered cherries for you, Jenny." "Oh, thank you," Jenny said as she took the box from him. She already missed the fudge; it was nothing like she had ever tried.

The baker walked through a door, and he was gone. James went to check it, and it was a closet. Jenny told James everything the shopkeeper had told her and showed him the large box of treats and lunch. James told Jenny he believed they had lived one of God's dreams for his people. James gathered the remaining package of gifts and goodies and took them to the car.

There were two cups of hot cocoa in Christmas travel cups for them. Jenny took the cups and went to the door; she glanced back to the living room and saw a card on the mantel. She walked over and took it. Jenny decided to wait and open it with James. She headed to the door, and the music from the radio stopped, and the announced time was twelve forty-five in the afternoon, and "Have Yourself a Merry Little Christmas" would be the last song of the day.

Jenny heard Jessica's voice saying, "Merry Christmas to all." James walked in and saw Jenny leaning against a beam facing the living room, holding the cocoas and a card.

"Are you ok," he asked? "Yes, I am. Just remembering the past few days once more before we leave, that's all." Jenny said.

James put his hands on her shoulders from behind and said, "It's possible, I believe."

Jenny turned to kiss James. "Thank you, she said, and I believe."

They walked out the door together. The car was all warmed up, and James had the GPS on. They both took a very long look at the cottage. Jenny handed James the card.

"What is this?"

Jenny told him she had found it, on the mantel with our names, so he opened it. Everyone in the village signed the card. They finished reading the card and looked up, and the cottage was gone. James laughed. "I hope we didn't forget anything."

Jenny slapped him on the arm, "That's a good one," she said.

They leaned to each other for a small kiss.

"Let's go," Jenny said.

They had a little over two hours left on their trip. It was quiet for a while when Jenny asked,

"It was real, wasn't it? I remember everything, and I believe it to be real."

James said, "Yes, it was real, and we're better together because of it. We have proof."

"What do we tell our friends," Jenny asked. James answered, "We're healed; that's enough. We don't owe any explanations to anyone. They will see a difference in us and be happy for us if they're our true friends and they won't ask questions."

"Let's not tell anyone about the village. Let's keep this very special secret between the two of us," Jenny recommended.

"Good idea, I like it," James said. Jenny grabbed James' hand.

"I'm hungry," said James. Jenny pulled out the sandwiches, and James found a rest stop so they could eat. They laughed and talked. They even started talking about starting a family sometime after the first of the year.

They passed a very nice lake, and it had a sign listing lots for sale. They stopped and took a number so they could check this place out on their way home. Jenny said, "It even said on one of the signs that there were finished homes for sale as well."

They both got very excited and talked about what kind of cottage they wanted to build.

"Log cabin for sure, five bedrooms and a massive fireplace. We can spend our summers and Christmas vacations here."

James asked, "Five bedrooms?"

"Right, we'll need that if we're planning to have children. Of course, we'll need a dog too, for the kids too," James added.

"A little dog, for the kids?" Jenny asked.

"Yes, dear," James answered.

It was like when they were first married. They were finally making plans and looking forward to their future together once again. The time passed so quickly they were so busy talking and before they knew it they were at the resort.

James checked in and apologized for being so late. The lady at the desk said she didn't know what he was talking about. They were right on time for their reservation. She asked the gentleman from the concierge desk to take them to their chalet. They got back in their car and followed him. The gentleman introduced himself as Nick, and he would help them for the rest of their stay.

Jenny and James elbowed each other and said, "What other name would he have," and they chuckled together.

He carried the bags. Then Nick gave James a card with his number on it. He left, and they were on their own.

The chalet was beautiful; it overlooked the mountains, with huge windows. They had a kitchen and an eating space down the stairs; the living room was open and large, with a big fireplace. Upstairs was a loft with a beautiful log-style bed and a bathroom with everything from a sauna to a hot tub.

"We don't need to leave; it's all here," James said.

He called to have dinner delivered around six that evening.

There was a knock at the door. It was Nick asking if they would like him to start a fire for them.

"Yes," was the unanimous answer.

Nick finished up and told them he would see them at six with their dinner. Jenny said she thought she would like to use the sauna, and James joined her.

They kept this time for total intimacy. They didn't even sign up for anything except a couple's massage, and those were done in the privacy of each chalet.

Each morning they opened the bakery box and had a breakfast sweet of some kind. They talked over and over about their great week and decided to go home a couple of days early. They were ready and excited about a cottage on the lake. They called and made an appointment with the realtor and stopped on their way home. It was like two kids looking at things for the first time. Land on waterfront lots and finished homes. There was a decision made. They would build. A two-acre waterfront lot with a mountain view was available, and they took it. The ground would break in spring, and it would be ready to live in or move in around Thanksgiving.

CHAPTER SEVENTEEN

They returned home and enjoyed a very intimate New Year's eve. The next day they spent it with family and friends. Everyone noticed a significant change in them, but no one ever asked. They were just happy to see them this way. Everyone knew that asking any questions would only open old wounds for Jenny, so they refrained from bringing it up. For the first time in a long time, they even played with their niece.

They opened up Toby's bedroom, took his rocking horse out into the family room next to the fireplace, and put the yellow quilt on it. His name was there for all to share in. Jenny placed the cowboy teddy bear on the quilt over the saddle. Jenny also took Toby's newborn photo, framed it, and hung it in the hall with the wedding photos. They painted and redid Toby's bedroom as well.

Jenny had promised to make it neutral and keep it open every day. Jenny often looked at her bracelet with a loving smile. She wore it every day. They started going to the gravesite again and telling Toby about their day. They shared their happiness for the time spent with the twins and the joy they had brought to them in those special couple of days.

Days passed by very quickly, and the improvement in both of them was quite visible. Valentine's day was approaching, and James was planning a romantic getaway for the two of them. Work had been very hectic ever since they got back, and Jenny had been writing a new children's book, which left them with very little time for each other.

She was super tired from all the editing and writing, and James was exhausted after work. They were ready to have a couple of days off.

Valentine's day is day after tomorrow and Jenny wasn't feeling well. A couple of people at work had the flu, so she decided to see her doctor the following day. She hated to tell James she had the flu, but she needed some help. They called the office and excused themselves for the day. James went with her because he thought he would be next to get sick, so he needed to know what to do to help.

The doctor had Jenny do blood work the day before. He knew he would have the results for a couple of things. Jenny and James sat in the room, her vitals were taken, and they waited for the doctor to come in.

While they waited, a lady brought a machine into the room, and she left without saying a word.

The doctor came in and said he had the results from the bloodwork.

Jenny asked, "What can I do for this flu?" The doctor chuckled and said, "It's not the flu, my dear, it's morning sickness, and you're having a baby."

"What!" James stood and shouted, "You're kidding. We weren't planning this yet. We haven't been trying."

The doctor looked at James and gave that odd look where a man does that thing with their eyebrows.

"But we haven't done anything to stop this either," James boasted.

He took a deep breath and pushed out his chest like a rooster. James babbled on, nonstop, "Wow, wow, Jenny, this is amazing!"

"Guess you'll have to change your plans," the doctor said as he just laughed.

"When, when is the baby due? What do we do next?" James asked earnestly.

"What do I do for Jenny?"

"Well," the doc said, "This machine will check out the heartbeat, and we'll get some pictures." James grabbed Jenny's hand, "Are you ok? Do you need anything?" he asked.

"Honey, I love you," Jenny finally spoke and said, "I'm fine. This is a miracle."

The doctor had questions about dates. Jenny and James were still in shock; they both started crying and hugging each other. The ultrasound machine was hooked up. The doctor asked Jenny to put on a hospital gown and lay down for him. The ultrasound was showing more than they ever expected. The doctor kept rubbing this one area, "Hmm," he kept saying.

Jenny said nervously, "We lost a baby just after he was born. I can't take the suspense. What's wrong?"

The doctor said, "Nothing's wrong; I just don't know how to tell you. He paused for a moment. You're having twins."

"Oh my!" Jenny cried out, and James was speechless. "James, did you hear that, two, two babies?" Jenny asked.

James just shook his head and cried. "Are Jenny and the babies ok?" he asked.

"Yes," the doctor said, "But we'll keep a very close eye on them. Lots of vitamins and good food. Now it's time to figure out how far along you are."

The doctor took measurements of the babies, and they got to hear the heartbeats. James and Jenny hugged through tears. The bloodwork told them more. "It looks like you're just shy of two months pregnant."

"Almost two months, that means Christmas Eve," Jenny said as she covered her mouth.

"Bingo," the doctor said, "That's what I needed to know."

"We had a full week of total intimacy every day," said James in a proud kind of way.

"James," Jenny whispered. "Jessica and Nick knew the whole time that this would happen so fast." The doctor just laughed and said, "We're good. I have all the information I need."

"Jenny, we will check with you again in three weeks. It looks like you'll be due in late August; we'll get a more exact date as we monitor you. Congratulations, mom, and dad!" the doctor said.

Jenny received some medicine for morning sickness. Still, in disbelief, they stopped to get a nice lunch. James told Jenny about the planned surprise getaway.

"Let's go, Jenny," he said, "We need this time alone. Let's wait and tell our families tomorrow.

We can enjoy this special day for ourselves" James and Jenny went home; while packing, Jenny remembered the Valentine gifts from Jessica that said "Open on February 14th."

She sat down on the couch, and James got the boxes out of the closet.

"I know tomorrow is the 14th, but I'm sure opening them today will be ok," Jenny said, and they both began to open them.

Jenny was overwhelmed by what she saw, two baby quilts, one blue and one pink, the ones she saw in the fabric shop. Timothy and Tomalina's names were sewn on them, and two baby outfits, one pink and one blue were inside the box. It was all hand crochet and looked beautiful.

She said, "This is what I wanted to give the new parents. Oh my! We're the parents!" she shouted as she pulled the items to her heart.

"That was us; we got to see our children!" She cried, and James hugged her.

"Tomalin called me mommy when she said goodbye," Jenny said.

James replied. "I never told you. Timothy called me daddy when he said goodbye."

Jenny started to laugh. Here we go, not telling each other something special, afraid to hurt the other one. James agreed they were a pair. Jessica and Nick knew the whole time; they agreed that they played a very special role.

Jenny and James called their parents on FaceTime and shared the good news with them the next day. Both their families were very happy and excited about the couple's new beginning. Jenny's mother asked if she needed any help to visit them both in the later months. James' parents offered the same. But they respected the couple's choice to spend the early days of Jenny's pregnancy alone.

James and Jenny stayed faithful to their promises to each other, always loving each other and never shutting down again. They set up Toby's old bedroom to receive his new baby brother and sister. They placed a picture of Toby in the bedroom. Jenny found a snowlady and put it on a shelf in the bedroom.

Twin babies were born in the middle of August with no health issues. Jenny and James asked not to know the gender of the babies in advance; well, they already knew.

One boy Timothy Nicholas and one girl Tomalina Jessica joined the Lucks family, August 15th. The entire family was there to welcome them to the family. Grandpas did what grandpas do. They told everyone they met in the hospital about the babies. Grandmas, well, you know what they did. Debbie and Jack announced they were having a second baby also. The twins stayed two extra days to undergo a battery of tests to ensure their health.

A package arrived in the mail shortly after Timothy and Tomalina came home from the hospital, James opened it up, and it was a baby doll with a pink lace dress and a little toy train engine. One more gift was also there, the book that Jenny read to Tommy. These are the toys the children had in the village. In the box was a nutcracker crib mobile, the same one Jenny had seen in the village woodshop.

They spent their first family Christmas in their new cabin on the lake. The one-of-a-kind tree topper had arrived and was placed at the top of the tree. Christmas music was playing in the background, and Jenny was singing along. This time it was because of pure happiness and for the children.

Jenny and James danced around the room to Christmas music as they did a year ago in the Christmas Cottage. They never forgot or shared how it all happened. Jenny and James never saw them, but Nick and Jessica watched the family together on Christmas Day through the topper on the tree. They smiled, and Jessica kissed Nick's cheek.

After a long break, Jenny started writing children's books again. She was content in life as her family was now complete once again, and good days were ahead of them.

She wrote a new series about a couple of mischievous twins. Both redheads with dark eyes, always into trouble and constantly exploring. Chocolate chip cookies, a little toy train engine, and a baby doll with a pink dress are written into every adventure of "Double Trouble."

Maddie and Max were added, a couple of small dogs for the kids, of course. One boy, and one girl, brother and sister, "Cocker spaniels."

Timmy and Tommy were three when the news about twins being born needed adoption. James and Jenny didn't have to think twice. They just said yes. The entire family was there when the new twins became members of "The Lucks Family." One boy Philip John and one girl, Piper Ann, added two new charms to the bracelet.

Each and every day was a new adventure with many blessings. Of course, Toby was still an important part of it all and was held in high regard in their memories. Jenny and James collaborated on a novel about a wild, unexpected snowstorm, a village, and its

"Enchanted Christmas Cottage."

THE END